Calamity.

Book one of Rage MC-The Prospects.

Elizabeth N. Harris

To Kerry,
Enjoy the book!
And keep those
tissues handy
Love
Elizabeth
ox

ISBN 9798367622768

This is a work of fiction. Names, characters, businesses, places, events, and incidents are either the product of the author's imagination or used in a fictitious manner. Any resemblance to actual persons, living or dead, or actual events is purely coincidental.

Elizabeth N. Harris
Calamity.
Book one of Rage MC-The Prospects

Cover by Joe Prachatree @
https://www.indiepremades.com/
Editor: Ellie Race
Proofreader: Jordan Howes.
Beta readers: Tammy Carney, Jayne Rushton, Natasha Kemmer, Jacqui Edge, Christy Pritchard, Kathy Jackson, Victoria Rae Stewart Hine and Julie McLain-Berger.

Calamity.

An abused child sought a home and discovered one in Rage MC. He was accepted, welcomed and finally found his place. He protected the old ladies, embraced Rages' values, and became their perfect prospect. Until the day he saw her. The Rage Princess nobody dared date. The moment he touched her, he knew she was his one. But they were too young, and he hadn't earned his way. So he bided his time.

No one was strong enough to stand up to her father. The couple of guys she'd introduced him to soon fled with their tails between their legs, so she gave up and concentrated on her education until him. His eyes made promises he couldn't keep yet, but they yearned for one another. She watched from afar, no one guessing her true feelings, until he brought an injured animal in and declared she was his.

He'd earned his patch, his role, and his respect. The day he became a brother was his proudest but not his best. The day he walked her down the aisle would be his best. As a brother, he could now claim the hand of the woman he loved. But nothing was ever going to be easy for him. Against the anger of family, disloyalty, and betrayal, can two souls find their path together, or will he do as he promises? And give his cut up for life.

Books by Elizabeth N. Harris

Rage MC series.

Rage of the Phoenix.
The Hunters Rage.
The Rage of Reading.
The Crafting of Rage.
Rage's Terror.
The Protection of Rage.
Love's Rage.
The Hope of Rage.
First Rage.
The Innocence of Rage.
The Sweetness of Rage.
The Range of Rage.
Rage's Model.
The Rage of Angels.
The Hell of Christmas Rage
The History of Rage

Rage MC – The Prospects

Calamity

Hellfire MC Series.

Chance's Hell.

The Savagery of Hell.
The Scream of Hell.
Justice of Hell.
The Horror of Hell.

Washingtons. *(Completed series)*

James.
Jaime.
Frankie.
Adam.

Love Beyond Death series. (*Completed series*)

Oakwood Manor.
Courtenay House.
Waverley Hall.
Corelle Abbey.
Eléonore Castle.
DeLacy Park.

Love Beyond Death – The Inns.

The Jekyll and Hyde.

Chapters.

Dedication.

To everyone who clamoured for Calamity's book, here you go. To Jacqui, who battles on despite personal tragedy and still remains a close friend and a much loved and valued beta reader. My respect and love to you always. To my friend Christy who always greets the day with a smile no matter what happens, this book is for you and Jordan. See you in Colorado, hun, and with that helicopter ride promised, just remind Matt!

This book is set during the pandemic. Rather than sidestep the entire issue, I have addressed it briefly during a passage with Calamity. These are his thoughts, as his character would have believed. Please do remember Calamity is fantasy; he doesn't exist as a real person. South Dakota was a state that did not have a mandatory lockdown, but after reading through various reports, many businessmen and individuals did what they could to lessen the spread of Covid in their state. But they did shut the schools and switch to online learning.

According to

https://www.worldometers.info/coronavirus/country/us/ the figures given for Covid-19 in the states are as follows. There have been 100,156,325 confirmed cases as of 19/11/2020. Out of those, 1,102,439 were confirmed deaths. In South Dakota, there have been 266,843 confirmed cases with 3088 confirmed deaths, according to https://doh.sd.gov/COVID/Dashboard.aspx. And in Pennington County, where Rage MC is based, there were 37441 confirmed cases and 367 confirmed deaths.

And the article, states, https://www.vox.com/future-perfect/2020/10/27/21534480/north-dakota-south-dakota-covid-coronavirus-pandemic-third-wave South Dakota was one of the worst states hit with Covid.

It is not my intent to give a political opinion on any of this, but Covid forms part of Calamity's story.

Love

Elizabeth x

Elizabethnharris74@outlook.com
Elizabethnharris.net
Sign up for my newsletter

This book was written, produced and edited in England, the United Kingdom, where some spelling, grammar and word usage will vary from US English.

A Quick Note!

After a couple of reviews and emails commenting on grammar and spelling errors, I thought I'd explain. My work is edited thoroughly, and some grammar and spelling will differ from US English. For example, color to colour or focusing instead of focussing. But I type as I imagine the characters to speak. I've been around several MCs and also know a good many bikers, and believe me, they don't watch their grammar! So you may find errors when one of the characters speaks; that's intentional! Even educated characters may drop their p's and q's from time to time, and we'll let them off because we love them so much!

Drake may use *don't* instead of *doesn't*, *it don't make* sense instead of *it doesn't make sense*. Or I *be* angry instead of *I am* angry! Or Phoe may say *me and you* instead of the grammatically correct *you and I*. They also drop words, possibly one of my own personal pet peeves! *You won't do it* becomes *won't do it*, or *it ain't right* turns into *ain't right*. However, typos are not deliberate, and if you find any, I sincerely apologise!

I hope you enjoy the book because I write from the heart and genuinely love my Rage MC characters and the world I'm creating around them.

Rage had failed in more ways than one.

Happy Reading!

Elizabeth N. Harris

Prologue

April 2020.

I arrived at Rage in September 2016, a broken, hungry kid who just wanted a chance. One chance to prove myself. Instead, I'd thrown my wallet at Drake, attempting to show I was a man. In that instant, Drake Michaelson saw me for what I was and sized me up. What surprised me was that he didn't find me wanting. I was barely nineteen and had a stupid hillbilly name of Billy Tomkins. I had no money, no education, nothing to offer Rage as Drake stared me down in the forecourt. He attempted to give me a nickname, Bane, Menace, Nightmare, all the names that asshole always called me.

Then Drake gave me a gift that no one else had. A name of my own. Calamity. It was mine; I claimed it, and I fuckin' earned it. Drake didn't stamp on the little pride I had left. He'd guessed I was homeless and offered me a bunk. And I swore then that a man who could leave me with my pride and dignity intact and not put me down deserved my loyalty. I'd shown that loyalty when I came to Silvie's rescue and took a beat down, saving her from a serial killer. That gained me prospect, and I was so damn proud. Nobody could say I hadn't proved my worth.

That act also got me a motorbike, one bought by Fish and designed by Jett. Fuck, I cried when I saw that beauty. That bike would go to the grave with me no matter what happened. Because it meant acceptance and love. Something I'd yearned for all my life. Even in my darkest days, I'd hoped for a family, and now I've got them, brothers and sisters.

I'd displayed my devotion and respect for Drake and Rage when they put me in the fuckin' ring with Rock and Gunner to teach me how to fight. They beat me down and built me up so that the next time I saved someone, I wouldn't get so hurt. I'd protect those women with my life if I had to.

And tonight, I became a full brother in Rage MC. Maybe now I could claim the girl who'd stolen my heart.

Chapter One.

Billy Tomkins. 1998. Aged one.

I'd already learned that crying brought nothing except angry faces, pain, and shouting. Sat in the cot, I waited patiently for someone to remember I was here. I was hungry. My little brain couldn't recall the last time I ate. But my belly growled and hurt, and I let out a whimper. A man rose above me, shrieking, and I felt the blow and the following agony. He threw me something, and I picked it up and shoved it in my mouth. It was food, but it did not taste good. I devoured it because who knew when I'd get my next meal?

Billy 2001. Aged four.

The children were mean here. They made fun of my clothes and hair. Dierdre, not Mom, she hated to be called that, had taken some scissors and given me an awful haircut. It was terrible, but Dierdre didn't care. Dierdre informed me this was school, and I'd have to visit every day. I was horrified and wondered if they'd discovered a new punishment. She and Clyde seemed to fight more, and I did everything to stay out of their way.

When the other children got their lunchboxes, I didn't have one and was confused. A teacher kept asking where my meal was, and I shrugged and said I never had much. Kindly she made a sandwich, gave it to me, and told me to bring lunch next time. I asked what that meant because I often went days without food. The teacher pulled a funny face and informed me she'd speak to someone.

That night, Clyde beat me black and blue, and I never returned for two weeks. Finally, a guy in a uniform came and demanded to see me. Truthfully, I was more scared of him than Clyde and refused to talk. The next day I was forced to return to school, but I had a lunch box now. Meals were something I didn't understand, and I asked the lady teacher many questions. An emotion shone in her eyes that made me squirm. But I was too young to pity.

Billy. 2005, aged eight.

Damn Clyde. He'd broken my arm in two places, and the hospital wouldn't let me go. Dierdre sat by my side, explaining I'd fallen from a tree, but the doctor was too suspicious. I'd been in the ER too many times. The doctor calmly informed Dierdre that child services were being called and security would detain her should she attempt to remove me. Once they'd left, Dierdre turned angry eyes on me and pinched my ribs. The witch didn't notice the nurse watching through the window.

Dierdre threatened me with far worse than the beating Clyde had dished out if I did not back up their story.

I shrugged. Hell, I'd undergone so many beatings; what was one more? Being beaten didn't matter. The pain came and then eventually left my tiny body. Yeah, I was underweight and undersized. Poor nutrition, yes, I knew that word. Despite missing days of school, I was clever and able to catch up and even was a little ahead of my classmates.

The teachers seemed amazed I could catch up so quickly after so much time off, but I always did. None questioned why I wasn't attending, although a few had seen bruises. Whether they'd been reported or not was a different matter. But tonight, this doctor stood up to Dierdre, and I wondered if I should blurt out the entire story. I was still considering my options when the doctor returned with a nurse. The nurse was glaring at Dierdre, and the doctor looked furious. Behind them came two hulking men.

"Mrs Tomkins, we'd like you to follow us, please," the doctor asked.

Dierdre sat up, putting on a confused expression. Avidly, I watched, wondering what was happening.

"Sorry, I can't leave Billy when he's in pain and scared!" Dierdre exclaimed.

Everyone sent me a look, and I stared back. Not afraid at all.

"Mrs Tomkins, you were witnessed threatening and pinching Billy. The police are on their way, and you are to be removed from Billy's vicinity," the doctor said firmly.

Dierdre let out an exaggerated cry, and her hand flew to her mouth.

"Who would say such horrible things?" Dierdre cried.

The nurse stepped forward.

"Me because I saw it. Billy, may I lift your top?" the woman asked kindly.

Deliberating, I glanced between her and Dierdre before nodding. As she lifted the tee, everyone could see the bright red mark on my ribs where Dierdre had pinched me. Deidre's face set, and she began loudly denying everything. It was funnier when Dierdre said I'd done it myself and broken my arm. No one believed the lying witch as she was dragged kicking and screaming from my room.

Perhaps good things would happen now.

Billy. 2006, aged nine.

I'd been home for three months, and I'd carefully observed Clyde and Dierdre during that time. Neither of them laid a hand on me, very aware of child services and the school hanging over their shoulder. Instead, the abuse turned mental. Clyde constantly screeched at me, calling me names, jinx, menace, and useless. Usually, I could ignore them, but they were settling into my bones.

My clothing was as poor as ever, either too short or too big. It all came from thrift stores or church jumble sales. No, I had nothing new. Even my trainers now had cardboard because there were holes in the soles, and they wouldn't buy me more. Squelching around with wet and cold feet hurt. School remained good and bad. Hell, I loved learning and soaked up everything I could. But I loathed the bullies who picked on me because of my clear level of poverty. Dierdre prepared a meagre lunch daily, the only meal I ate. No breakfast or dinner. Truthfully, I hated my parents and wished they would just up and die.

The children's home I'd spent six months in had been warm and clean, and while I still had nothing new, it had all been of excellent quality. In that place, I'd finally found happiness, which in my mind was plain sad. But after Dierdre and Clyde had completed the classes required to be good parents, I'd been returned. There'd been no point kicking off. The decision had been made. And the abuse turned from visible to invisible, but no less damaging.

Each day I left by seven. I hated being there when they woke up, and with the cupboards locked, I couldn't eat. There was no need to hang around.

Today, as I walked across the road to start my journey to school, my name being called loudly made me jump.

Oh no, no.

"Billy Tomkins, come here!" It was the dragon. Mrs Travis. Everyone in the street was afraid of her. Her house was supposedly haunted, and she never mixed with anyone in the community. Mrs Travis had one of those typical haunted houses, curtains closed, and while it looked well kept, it had a false air of neglect and being unloved. Neighbourhood kids claimed they'd seen strange lights and even ghosts there. Scared, I hesitated, not knowing whether to run, and Mrs Travis took the decision out of my hands.

"Billy Tomkins, I said right now, before I call the police and say I caught you trespassing." That made me glower. Just another adult ready to bully and threaten. Angry, I stomped to the front door, where Mrs Travis regarded me.

"Inside," she stated, and I did as I was told. Shivering, I stood in the warmth of the house and allowed it to seep into my bones. It was winter, snow was on the ground, and the thin summer jacket did little to keep me warm.

"Follow me, boy," Mrs Travis ordered, and I walked sullenly to a bright kitchen. "Sit!"

"Ain't done nothing wrong, Mrs Travis," I replied as

she glowered, and I sat quickly. No lie. Her reputation was terrifying.

"When's the last time you ate Billy Tomkins?" Mrs Travis demanded. Startled by the question, I frowned and stared. "Not that limp sandwich your so-called mother sends you with. A proper breakfast or meal?"

"Never," I muttered.

"Thought so. Now we don't want to make you sick, so sit there, boy, and eat this," Mrs Travis said, placing a bowl of porridge in front of me. Moments later, a mug of tea was placed next to it. I stared at it, wondering what the catch was. Mrs Travis watched as I sat and gawked at the bowl and mug.

"Billy Tomkins, eat your breakfast," Mrs Travis stated in a gentler tone.

Confused, I picked up the spoon, ready to duck if she aimed a blow at me and, to my surprise, Mrs Travis let me eat. Puzzled about what was going on, I ate rapidly, the warm food the first I'd eaten in a long time. Mrs Travis made me jump as she placed two pieces of toast in front of me, thick with butter. My eyes widened, and I grabbed them and chewed quickly.

"Billy, you need to learn manners, boy."

"Thank you, Mrs Travis," I said and flinched as her hand lifted.

Mrs Travis froze and then brushed the hair out of my face.

"Every day, I expect you here at seven. You'll shower and wash upstairs and put on the clothes I give you. In return, you will excel at school. Billy, I shall provide a nutritious breakfast for you; nothing too rich until you become used to eating properly. And you can throw that weak assed sandwich out to the birds in my yard. Boy, I'll make you a hearty lunch, and when you return from school, you'll do your homework here and eat a dinner I'll cook. Before you leave, you'll change into the clothing your damned parents have given you. Am I clear?" Mrs Travis said firmly.

"Why?" I demanded, wondering what the plan was. Did Mrs Travis want to fatten me up and kill me?

"Because Billy Tomkins, I was the one who called child services when you were taken to hospital with the broken arm. And I was appalled they returned you after Dierdre and Clyde snowballed them. So, I am taking matters into my own hands. Dierdre and Clyde will not wish to upset me. So, I shall take care of you as I see fit. You'll get an excellent education, Billy Tomkins, and be successful in your life. Now run upstairs, shower quickly, and dress in the clothes I've laid out. Lunch will be here when you return," Mrs Travis said.

I paused, confused and worried. Would this be when Mrs Travis turns on me like everybody else? Mrs Travis's eyes softened.

"Billy, we can't save everyone in the world. But when you can save one person, step up and do so. Go shower, and use as much hot water as you wish, but don't dawdle. No being late for school," Mrs Travis chided.

Without a word, I hurried to obey.

Billy. 2010, aged thirteen.

"I'm home, Mrs Travis!" I shouted, walking into the warm house.

"In here, Billy," she called back from the kitchen.

Happily, I headed in that direction and stopped when I saw Dierdre sitting there glowering. "What's going on?" I asked, stepping to Mrs Travis's side.

"Oh, your mother wanted a few words. Unfortunately, it hasn't gone how Dierdre desired," Mrs Travis said blithely.

Fear rose inside me as I noticed the hate in Dierdre's eyes.

"Huh?" I stuttered the word.

"Yes, Dierdre thinks she should be entitled to some of your good fortune. After four years, Dierdre just realised I've been caring for you. So, she came with her greedy, grabby hands out. So far, we've talked about me giving her a weekly bonus, as I clearly want you. Then we had the threats about siccing child services on me, as it's unnatural for a woman my age to look after a youngster.

"Then the physical intimidation began, followed by blackmail and threatening to tarnish my reputation. Dierdre didn't realise that I've been acting on your behalf since you were nine and have dealt with any schooling or other issues. There are multiple witnesses that I have been your guardian and that

Dierdre and Clyde still harm you. Oh yes, I'm well aware of the mental abuse they both heap on you. And I've started seeing the occasional bruise on your body again, Billy," Mrs Travis spoke with plain anger.

Dierdre scowled.

"You want him, then I'll take one hundred thousand for him," Dierdre snarled, and I rocked. Fuck, I knew she hated and didn't care for me, but to sell me?

"Deirdre, I'll pay nothing for the boy. Claimed Billy four years ago, and he's mine. However, I'll ensure that the police and child services don't return to you again. You and Clyde will stop all abuse towards Billy and leave him alone. We shall maintain our current status quo. Because cross me, Dierdre, and that'll be a big mistake. I have more power than you know, and life will become complicated," Mrs Travis announced calmly. It was even more chilling because she was so calm about it.

"Bitch, you're threatening me?" Dierdre hissed.

"Pointing out a fact. Try me because you won't like what happens next," Mrs Travis said. Fear turned to terror as Dierdre rose to her feet.

"We'll see," Deirdre spat.

"Dierdre, South Dakota is a one party permission to being recorded state. The moment you set foot in my home; you were on camera. Check and mate," Mrs Travis declared.

Dierdre froze as she clearly recalled their conversation. "You fuckin' bitch!" Dierdre shrieked.

"Leave my house. Billy will sleep at yours each

night. The remainder of his time, Billy stays with me."

Stunned, I watched as the woman who had birthed me stormed out.

"This isn't over," I said to Mrs Travis.

"For now, it is. Don't you have homework?"

Billy. 2015, aged eighteen.

My head was ducked down as Clyde heaped abuse on me. If not for Mrs Travis, I probably would have cracked by now. Mrs Travis's endless love and patience offset the hate and bitterness Clyde and Dierdre threw daily at me. I constantly remained on edge, in a state of perpetual alertness. A year ago, Mrs Travis had weakened. It made little sense; Mrs Travis was only sixty-five, not old. But she rapidly lost strength, and Clyde picked up on it. The beatings began again, and this time Clyde used weapons, knowing I wouldn't upset Mrs Travis.

Today Clyde had swung at me with a chain, and I'd wrapped it around his throat and choked him out. When Clyde passed out, I stared at him and Dierdre and told them I was done being their whipping boy. Terrified, I fled the house and headed towards Mrs Travis. As I entered the backdoor, I found the home strangely silent. Something was wrong. The oven was off. No mugs or cups were out for tea, and when I called her name, she didn't reply.

Quietly, I moved through the house until I came to the hallway, where I stared in horror. There, lying crumpled at the bottom of the stairs, was Mrs Travis, who was clearly dead. I didn't need to check because of the way her neck had twisted. She'd fallen down the stairs during the night because she wore her nightclothes. In the far distance, sirens screamed, and I turned my head. Had Deirdre and Clyde called the cops on me? If they found me here with Mrs Travis dead, would they arrest me? Shit, I didn't want to go to jail for something I hadn't done.

I bent down and kissed Mrs Travis on the forehead. It was cold and clammy, and I shuddered. Then I rushed to the room I used as my own and took the three thousand dollars I'd saved. And then, with one last look at the place I'd called home, I fled before I was wrongly arrested.

Calamity 2016, aged 19.

"Hey," a soft voice said, and I looked up and noticed Rosie standing beside me. Rosie jerked her chin downwards, and I grinned as I saw the two smuggled beer bottles. Rosie was old enough to drink now, but Texas kept a sharp eye on her. And I had a year until I was legal. Rosie tilted her head to a bench near the edge of the clubhouse, and I rose and followed her. I liked the view from the back. Rosie's hips gently flared, leading to a pert ass and long legs. Hell, I loved the view from the front just as much.

Rosie was classically beautiful. She had brown hair and a sweetheart-shaped face with her father's jawline, although it was gentler on her. Rosie's cheekbones were high, and there was no denying whose child she was when you looked into her piercing brown eyes. She most definitely had her dad's eyes.

I sent a quick look around for Texas but couldn't see him. Texas had no idea of my attraction to his daughter, and I intended to keep it that way.

Rosie was too good for me. Texas had raised Rosie right. She was at university, studying to be a vet. Me, I wasn't even worth calling trailer trash. Shit, I was below that. The stench of being the lowest of the low would forever remain. But for tonight, I could enjoy the company of a beautiful girl and forget I was ever Billy Tomkins.

Rosie 2017

Beyond furious, I stormed out of the library with a crowd on my heels and not by choice. That bloody idiot Rex had tried cornering me again, and a scene had eschewed. It was two weeks until Christmas break, and I couldn't wait to get away from Rex and his minions. Mr Popular on campus, Rex, had become the bane of my life. Tragically, we'd met at a party, and Rex had offered me an evening of fun. A huge target appeared on my back when I'd told Rex no. Rex had never been told no, and I triggered something vile and twisted inside him.

At first, Rex thought I was teasing. He kept trying to pin me against the wall that night, and as soon as I could escape, I did. Somehow Rex found out what dorm I was staying in and when I returned from class the following day, to my horror, he'd been waiting for me.

Rex tried a cheesy smile and weak obnoxious compliment and asked me out for drinks. The way Rex's eyes roamed my body let me guess correctly; the asshole wanted more than a drink.

I let Rex down gently, explaining I had homework to do, but Rex didn't care about that. He kept pushing until I firmly told him I wasn't interested. And hell, I'd waved a red flag at a bull. I escaped that night, but Rex turned up at my classroom with some of his suck-ups the following day. I was appalled at how they behaved and quickly left to find my next lesson. This became a game of either Rex or one of his hangers-on following me.

It had reached the stage where Rex's shit was frightening, and I'd put in a complaint. Friends began dropping away, and I'd gone from being an extrovert to an introvert in a matter of mere months. I'd been to the campus police, and Rex and his gang claimed I was encouraging them. The police, luckily, had believed my roommate and me as we'd kept diaries, and Rex was given a warning. A restraining order had been issued, but Rex wasn't obeying. Today I would meet with my professor to see what could be done. I didn't want to change colleges, but it appeared I'd have to.

The next step would be to contact Dad and Uncle Drake. They wouldn't be too amused at me being messed with in college. But I was trying to be an adult and handle this myself. Although I was a Daddy's girl, I did want to stand on my own two feet. Blame that stubborn streak of mine!

Anyone else would have backed off. No, not fucking Rex. He came after me twice as hard. It had got to the stage where I was a nervous wreck and rarely left the dorms except for lessons. I'd spoken to Jodie, Drake, and Phoe's daughter this weekend, and she said Rex was amping up for something. Rex's behaviour was dangerous.

Today, Rex caught me in the library and had been more handsy than usual. A fight had broken out between us when I slapped his hands away. Rex had crowded into my space and threatened me, groping my breasts and tearing my skirt as he attempted to lift it. I punched him straight in the nose and fled with Rex and his little gang behind me. As I raced out the library doors, I was startled to hear a Harley roaring up, and a biker I knew very well stopped in front of me.

"Rosie?" Calamity asked as Rex and his five buddies scrambled to a stop at the top of the stairs.

"Calamity! What are you doing here?" I gasped, keeping my body turned so I could see Rex from the corner of my eye.

"Was passing and thought I'd pop in. Texas said you'd be studying, so I took a chance and came straight to the library," Calamity answered. His eyes narrowed on my ripped skirt and then on Rex. "Looks like I was just in time."

"No, everything is fine. Why don't you meet me at my dorm, and we can eat?" I suggested quickly, trying to head off trouble.

Calamity had filled out since the attack on Silvie a year ago. The thin, underweight boy now had lean muscle and strength. Calamity may still have been twenty, but his frame was good after proper care and attention. Calam, as I called him, was nobody to be messed with. And while it would take Calamity a few years to mature into the threat Dad and my uncles posed... he was halfway there.

His gaze calmly focused on Rex and his friends, and I knew Calamity was gearing up.

"A meal sounds good, but I ain't meeting you nowhere. Climb up, baby girl," Calamity offered.

"Calam, I can't do that. Only your old lady will ride behind you," I exclaimed.

"Rosie, not telling you twice. Get on, or I'll put you there," Calamity replied firmly.

There it was. The hint of Rage implacability, the core strength that all Rage males gained. I was facing a member of Rage MC, not a friend or someone I secretly crushed on. No, I was staring at a Rage brother with all the threats and danger that came with him. Rex and his buddies suddenly seemed to realise that as the air of danger that rolled off Calamity hit them. They looked amongst themselves and disappeared into the library.

"Rosie," Calamity growled.

With a resigned sigh, I threw my leg over the motorbike and hung on tightly. Of course, it didn't hurt that I was pressed against Calamity. The smile on my lips gave away my feelings as the bike roared and we pulled off.

Calamity.

I was waiting in the darkness for the little fucker who thought he could bully a Rage princess. No fucking chance. I'd dragged the story out of Rosie reluctantly and what steps she had taken, and it was as clear as fuck that this asshole had an issue. I called Micah, Drake's son, to help, and the pair of us waited for this Rex. Obviously, we hadn't let Rosie know our plan; hell, Rosie wasn't even aware Micah was on campus. Micah was slightly older than me, but we'd bonded as brothers, and I knew he'd have my back.

Rosie had explained she didn't want Texas or Rage to know. That she was trying to be an adult and stand on her own two feet. However, that didn't stop me from planning to give this asshole a beatdown. Micah and I just wouldn't tell anyone about it. The motherfucker would get our message and Rosie could breathe freely.

Nobody messed with a Rage princess, nor the girl I

one day intended to claim as my own. Micah noticed how I felt about her, but we didn't discuss it. It was a sin of the highest order for a prospect to put his sights on a princess. When I had my full patch, then I'd claim Rosie. I'd protect her from anybody who thought they could mess with her. Micah tracked Rex to a bar, and we watched and waited. I'd tried hard not to laugh because somehow Micah had also got his hands on a jammer, which would block all cameras and phone signals. There'd be no comeback on us tonight.

The asshole messing with my girl staggered out of the bar with three of his friends. I recognised them all and nodded to Micah. Quietly, keeping in the shadows, we followed them until they cut down an alley, which was their mistake. Four big brave men. No one would hurt them. Micah pulled his handgun, and I stepped out and stopped them.

"What the fuck, asshole?" Rex drunkenly slurred.

"This is for Rosie," I growled and proceeded to beat him.

Rex's mates roared and moved to attack when they heard the click of a gun. Lifting their gazes, they saw Micah holding them hostage, and they pissed their pants. They all placed their hands in the air as I broke bones and tore skin, giving a motherfucking asshole a lesson he'd never forget. Rosie was off limits. When I finished with Rex, I beat each of his cock sucking friends the same. No one would forget the message I was sending.

When I was done, Micah looked me over and

smirked. "Wouldn't have been possible a year ago," the prick declared.

I laughed as we sprayed everything down with bleach, including those lying on the ground.

"They won't ever harass a woman again, not without looking over their shoulder," I muttered.

I kicked the boy called Rex in the head one more time before Micah and I left. On the way home, I burnt the clothes I had been wearing, the balaclava I'd worn, the gloves, and my boots. I put on fresh everything and rode back to Rage.

Rosie was safe.

After that, I made a point of dropping in each week on different days to check how Rosie was and to ensure she was left alone. I didn't see any of the assholes I'd put the beat down on for six weeks, but Rosie had been full of gossip about it. Rosie remained unaware it had been Micah and me. She'd informed me it was all over campus that Rex and his friends had tried fighting off a gang of guys who'd attacked a girl. But she announced it had been proven a complete lie as a camera had shown two men stalking them.

Guess I hadn't hit the jammer early enough, but there was still nothing to identify us. Micah and I had been dressed in black with balaclavas and left no DNA. Rosie was full of glee at how they'd been beaten and then proved liars. Even better, they were informed that they wouldn't be allowed to return to college because of Rosie's harassment at the end of the term.

To my amusement, I also discovered Micah was monitoring Rosie, visiting once a week. We were taking it in turns to show that Rosie was not unprotected in case any other asshole got ideas. So twice a week, Rosie got taken out for a meal and Micah and I ensured she had a great evening. I wasn't worried about Micah poaching my girl, because Micah knew how I felt, and he'd respect that. He was my brother.

Rosie

I wondered if Calamity and Micah thought I was that daft and naïve. The moment the news hit campus about the attack on Rex and his friends, I guessed who was behind it. Calamity had pried deeply that night to gain information to take matters into his own hands. I'd seen the light of ownership and possessiveness flare in his eyes. Calamity was not about to let anyone hurt me. And no surprise that where Calamity was, up turned Micah, and they both watched over me. At least it wasn't as dire as my father. As Secretary and Treasurer for Rage, Dad had more than enough clout to have someone put on me permanently.

Which was my worst nightmare. Nope, Calamity and Micah twice a week wasn't a bad thing. After witnessing the anger and then worry in Calamity's eyes, I recognised he truly cared for me, and not as a Rage princess. Calamity wanted me, but I knew how the club worked. A prospect couldn't claim me. Calamity was busting his balls to claim his patch, and then he'd claim me one day. And I was happy enough to wait.

Chapter Two.

April 2020.

Calamity

The clubhouse was packed and had been since six that evening. First, it had been the old ladies and kids celebrating my promotion to full patch, and then at nine, the skanks arrived. I'd never been one for club whores and wasn't about to start. No, my attention was taken by a curvy figure and long brown hair. Rosie's amber eyes followed me as I watched her. There was a secret smile on her lips. Yeah, I liked to think it was because I could now make a move. Rosie stood with Jodie, Serenity, and Willow, and they gossiped between themselves. Those four women were the oldest princesses, yet despite doting fathers, each remained independent.

"How's it feel?" Klutz asked, throwing an arm over my shoulder.

"Good. Feels like home," I replied, moving my gaze from Rosie before someone picked up on it.

"Did great, kid," Klutz spoke with a grin. I elbowed Klutz.

"You're not much older, a few years, remember that," I teased, and Klutz nodded. I felt his body become stiff as a tiny package of dynamite entered the club, and I followed his stare. Aurora Victoria was even more of a princess than the four I'd just mentioned. A founder's granddaughter. She'd appeared last year and was kidnapped and held hostage until Mac's woman, Casey, broke them out and blew the fuck out of the kidnappers. Not somebody to be messed with, Casey, as she was trained along the lines of Artemis.

"You're interested," I muttered, lowering my voice. Rage had a strict policy. Princesses were off-limits to hang-arounds, candidates, and prospects. Except I wasn't now and could claim Rosie, and I intended to do just that. I'd loved Rosie for years and had struggled to keep my hands to myself.

When Rosie had been attacked by the asshole stalking her, she'd given me an opening into her life, and I'd barged my way in. Rosie had never slammed the door shut, and it remained open. It would have been easy for Rosie to call Texas and complain about the prospect and his best friend bugging her weekly.

But Rosie happily took mine and Micah's protection, and Micah had admitted she often asked questions about me. Which told me everything I needed. Rosie was as into me as I was her. Instead of leaping on her, getting my ass beaten and then kicked from Rage, I played the long game.

Rosie and I built a friendship first, getting to know the ins and outs of each other. The relationship steadily grew from wary trust to calling one another for a chat. We both enjoyed our weekly date when we had a decent meal and a walk. Those hours to me were more precious than even my cut. I should be ashamed of saying that, but it was true. I loved Rosie more than anything in my life. And now I could claim her.

"Don't say a fuckin' word," Klutz hissed and grabbed my attention.

"About you and Aurora. Never. Be warned, brother, claiming a founder's legacy princess will be harder than the challenge I face," I murmured.

Klutz shot me a look before nodding.

"It's time?" he whispered.

"Yeah, I've proved my worth to Rage. There shouldn't be a barrier apart from Texas being over-protective. I can handle that. Rosie and I have been building something. She knows what I want and what my plan is. But it doesn't mean I'm going to rush shit. Steady as it goes. Texas will need to get his head around it," I replied, unsurprised Klutz had picked up on my feelings for Rosie.

While Klutz was a great barman, and loved to

perform tricks, which brought the ladies into the club-owned bar in swarms, he was also astute and alert. Klutz had divulged he'd been in his fourth year of medical school when he'd been wrongly arrested. By the time Klutz's innocence had been proved, his life lay in ruins. His family disowned him. He'd have to repeat his final year and then spend at least three years as a resident. Klutz had lost everything. Instead, Klutz had become a bartender before landing on Rage and finding a replacement family.

Much the same as me, Klutz didn't want to jeopardise what he had as he was frightened of losing his new family. Neither of us wanted to rock the boat, and I recognised many of my secret fears hidden within Klutz. No, he wouldn't move on Aurora until he was fully patched in.

"Bide your time," I muttered, and Klutz nodded and then stiffened. The club doors opened, and the whores waltzed in. Both of us cursed under our breaths and swapped a resigned glance.

The skanks came with the club. Single men fucked them, while married and taken ones stayed away. No piece of ass was worth sabotaging what they had with their old ladies. And I tried to stay clear of them too. Who wished to go where his brother's dick had dipped? Or sink into a brother's cum. The idea disgusted me. I'd had a couple of one-night stands and picked up women from the bar, but when I'd set sights on Rosie, my right hand and cock were soon well acquainted. It had been three years since that decision to make Rosie mine, and I'd not fucked a woman since.

If people discovered that, I'd have eye rolls. I was a man, a brother, and a biker. I screwed who and when I wanted. Which was my point. I did not want to fuck any of them, so I didn't. I only needed one lady. Rosie. My love had such strength for her that I could easily do without sex. Mrs Travis had drummed into me that if you really loved someone, you'd wait for them to be ready. You didn't need cheap and meaningless sex to prove you were a man. A real man realised what he wanted and waited to achieve his goal. There was no way I would ever prefer to take a plethora of women to bed with me when I claimed Rosie.

Some of my brothers were male whores. Lex and Mac had recently settled down, and they'd been two of the worst. Ezra still wasn't picky about who he fucked. Only Ezra, Slick, Manny, and Slate remained single out of the fully patched men. Then we had the prospects: Tye, Carmine, Savage, Klutz, Gauntlet, and Harley. Plus, the candidates, Wild and Cowboy and Ellen would kill any skank who touched her baby boys, much to their amusement. Wild and Cowboy were finding out quickly what a genuine mother meant. And were overwhelmed by it, although entertained.

"If she fuckin' comes near me tonight," Klutz muttered, and I looked up. Three of the skanks, tits and ass hanging out and makeup pancaked on, were looking in our direction.

From the ten that visited regularly, these three

bitches were aggressive in attempting to catch a brother. They had made the mistake of touching a taken husband. Which Artemis, Lindsey, and Autumn soon discouraged, alongside the brother's old lady. Hell, it was only a few months ago Artemis and Autumn had laid the law down after beating the crap out of two skanks. The rules were clear. Any brother who claimed a woman was immediately off-limits. They did not cheat and hated being forced into a position where they had to defend themselves and their relationship.

If they'd put their name on a woman's back, it meant they were committed to her and didn't appreciate anyone calling their integrity into question. Which had become open season on those of us left single. I spent more time ducking the whores than I did drinking and relaxing. Charley, Liza, and Trudi turned in our direction, and a groan escaped my mouth. Without realising it, I sent a panicked, silent look for help at Rosie and braced as the skanks wandered over with hideous grins on their lips.

"Fuck!" I moaned as Klutz tensed.

Charley pasted herself to my side as I moved away and stepped straight into Liza's clutches.

"Take your hands off me," I growled.

Charley pouted as she came closer. Out of the corner of my eye, I saw Klutz fending Trudi off.

"Come on, Calamity, we're celebrating, aren't we? You becoming a fully patched member is huge!" Liza drawled.

"Not with you. Said I'm not interested. Find

someone who is," I retorted and hissed as Liza cupped my dick.

"Honey, we can make tonight memorable." Liza smiled.

"Get your fuckin' hands off me. I've told you plenty of times, now fuck off!" I snapped, my temper rising as I twisted away.

Klutz was saying much the same and holding Trudi at arm's length. The smell of roses filled my nose, and Rosie appeared and glared at the two skanks. Beside her came Jodie and Serenity while Aurora Victoria stood in front of Klutz with a dark look, and Willow was by her side.

"Calamity said fuck off, do so," Rosie yelled.

Silence fell over the room as the brothers suddenly realised the princesses were having a showdown.

"And Klutz said the same. Go find some other poor schmuck to screw!" Aurora snapped.

"Who do you think you're talking to?" Liza growled.

I groaned, rubbing a hand down my face. Disrespect towards an old lady was a reason for a beat-down. To show a lack of respect to a princess? Worse happened.

"I'm speaking to someone who only knows the language of being on her knees sucking cock. However, these two have made it very plain they don't want your herpes-filled body anywhere near them. Take your STDs and walk away. Now!" Rosie seethed.

"Rosie?" Texas called as he approached at speed.

"You can't talk to me like that!" Trudi screeched.

"Bitch, she wasn't talking to you. How thick are you? Did you blow all your brain cells sucking cock?" Aurora asked bitchily, and I hid a smile.

Trudi let out an outraged shriek. Her hand came up, and she aimed a slap at Aurora, who didn't flinch. Before the smack landed, Klutz charged and had Trudi by the throat and was lifting her off the floor.

"You don't lay a fuckin' finger on a princess!" Klutz roared.

Liza, ignoring the scene and the consequences so far, slapped Rosie before I could intercept. Rosie's head moved at the force of the slap, and then she slowly turned and stared at Liza, who gulped in the sudden silence. Without a word, Rosie stepped forward and smashed Liza straight in the nose. We all heard it break, but Rosie wasn't Texas's daughter for nothing. Raining blows and kicks, Rosie silently beat Liza to the ground and finished her with a kick to the head. Not even panting, Rosie faced Charley, who paled and held her hands up.

"Klutz, let the bitch go before she chokes out," Drake said quietly.

Klutz shook Trudi one more time before releasing his grip, and Trudi fell to the floor, gasping and clutching her throat.

I moved Rosie behind me as I faced Charley.

"No one touches a princess. Not a single fuckin' person. Get your shit, pack their crap up, and get the fuck off Rage. If Klutz or I see you here or in town, you'll disappear without a trace. The rest of you bitches," I snarled and turned to the watching skanks, "you try to force your attention on a brother again, and it won't be the wives and daughters of Rage you need to worry about. I kept quiet because I was a prospect and not a brother.

"But I'm sick of how you try to push your way into our beds. You ain't gonna get an old lady patch. None of us wishes to parade around a woman our brothers have already fucked. You chose this existence. Rage didn't force you. But you can't seriously think we'd pick you for the back of our bikes. We got more self-respect than that to bring such dishonour to our bike. You're here to screw if we want to fuck, not for you to catch a brother by his balls. Know your place. You are whores, nothing more, nothing less. And if I ever see you disrespect an old lady or princess again, you'll dig your own grave."

Wide eyes stared in horror as I laid the law down. Some prospects, Tye and Carmine for two, nodded happily while Ezra and Manny glowered at the women.

"They've been getting too big for their boots," Slick announced. "I woke the other day to find Charley had climbed into my bed during the night uninvited. Drake, I think it's time we took a vote on whether we have them keep coming around. If a brother wants to get laid, he can pick one up in town or at the bar. This easy pussy is just fuckin' awkward with the kids." Several nods met Slick's words, although he was a single man.

"We'll bring it up in church," Drake promised and

turned away. "Someone put the music back on. This is a celebration."

The volume rose in the clubhouse.

I snatched Rosie to my side and ducked my head.

"Thank you. I'm so sick of those bitches," I whispered in her ear.

Rosie shuddered, and a warm feeling welled inside me. Rosie wasn't immune at all.

"It's about time they were voted out. What you said is correct. There is no need for them. How soon before one of the kids witness something? Or a fuckin' bimbo tries to come between a married couple?" Rosie spat, and I noticed the whores were grating on her nerves.

"Rosie, you know I've not touched one of them? Not since the day I set sights on you." Rosie's body jolted, and she turned disbelieving eyes on me.

"You don't need to lie about being with them, Calamity. Every brother has fucked them or someone like them," she replied softly.

"Rosie, the moment I saw you, I knew you were the one. But you were studying to be a vet, and I was a mere candidate. I had nothing to offer you back then, and you had the world at your feet. The decision to sit and watch from afar was hard, but I swore then you were the only lady for me. So I did the decent thing and waited, knowing you'd be mine one day. Understanding I loved you meant no other woman interested me or my dick. I've slept with three women before seeing you and none since. And if you doubt me, ask around, baby. No one can say they witnessed

43

me take a skank to my bunk. And the bunk is the only home I have," I said earnestly.

"Calamity," Rosie breathed, and I smiled. My words had hit just like I wanted.

"It's you and always will be you, baby. Why do you think Micah and I kept coming to ensure you were safe? Rosie, your safety and happiness meant more than anything, and now I'm a full brother; I can offer you a decent life. Can give you everything your heart desires," I promised.

"What's going on here? This looks serious?" Texas boomed, interrupting us and throwing an arm around Rosie. Texas stared between us with an uplifted eyebrow.

"We were discussing the skanks and how disrespectful and disruptive they are, Dad," Rosie said quickly.

Texas's brows settled into a frown. "Whores are club business," Texas replied.

"Yup, because us women have no feelings about them, nor are we allowed any!" Rosie snapped, and amusement rose.

"Hey, I didn't say that," Texas cried.

"Yeah, you did. Whores are club business. Because it's your dicks getting wet by them. Doesn't matter that Rage old ladies or the princess get hurt by them, does it? Nope, as long as your cocks get sucked," Rosie spat, and I tried to hide a smile.

Texas appeared blown off his feet by Rosie's attitude.

"Rosie," Texas growled.

I became alert. No way would I allow Texas to blast

Rosie, daughter or not.

"Dad," Rosie mocked. "You not noticed Penny is barely eating? One whore was calling Penny fat and making bets about when you'd start gracing their beds. Penny was deeply hurt, and because whores are off-limits, we're unable to talk to you about it. That's why Penny's been starving herself to lose weight because she is frightened of losing you.

"And what about the skanks that approach the princesses and diss us to our faces? They say hurtful things about our fathers and how they liked to screw them. And we have to suck it up because, hey, skanks are the club's business. Who gives a shit about wives and princesses? The old ladies have it good. Hell, they get your precious cocks, so they should be grateful. Bull-fucking-shit. And the princesses are so overly protected it's a fuckin' miracle we're allowed off-site. Your shit about whores being club business is bullshit, and it is time to wake up and face it."

I was proud of Rosie because I agreed with everything she said, but she wasn't stopping. Once again, silence had fallen as brothers tuned in. Drake glowered, and Rosie squared her shoulders. She was not backing down.

"Rosie, you know they are club business," Drake said in a dark tone.

Rosie released an evil little smile that made me very wary. "Club business when they make my stepmother starve herself because she believes she'd lose Dad's love and attention? Bullshit. How about when they make fun of Ellen because of her age and

45

said she can't keep Axel happy, and it won't be long before he's poking one of them?"

A boom of disgust came from Axel.

She continued, "Oh, they say it to Ellen's face, don't worry."

"Why haven't you said anything?" Axel boomed at Ellen.

She shrugged.

"Because, as Drake says. It's club business. Nobody cares the skanks disrespect us. No, you all stand there amused when we beat them down. But the main reason we beat them is that they hurt us, and it's overlooked," Autumn spoke up.

Gunner glowered. "They've said shit to you?"

"Oh, I know how you liked to screw them and loved your blowjobs. How you enjoyed banging two together. They swear that when my body doesn't bounce back as it used to from having your kids, they'll have you in their beds. And why shouldn't I believe them? You all still have them hanging around. You'd go nuts if I had a guy I fucked come here. None of you wants to be confronted by our past lovers, and yet every day we face these skanks knowing you all screwed them," Autumn said bitterly.

"But it's okay because, hey, they rank above our feelings. And they are club business. They nearly killed Silvie and Halona. Because they wanted to claim Ace back for themselves. One of them hid Silvie's phone, so she couldn't call for aid, and Silvie was in so much pain she couldn't walk to get help.

But they're still hanging around despite nearly killing an old lady."

Artemis sat glowering at the skanks congregating together.

Anger hit as I realised how smug some of them looked. The old ladies were right. The whores needed to go.

"You have no say in who single brothers fuck. Club sluts have always been a part of MC life," Drake retorted.

I winced and shot Phoe a glance, watching as she climbed to her feet at Drake's words. The shit was about to hit the fan.

"So, it's okay when whores say they ain't going to help clean up around here, that it's our job to cook and tidy for you all? Despite the fact we all work full-time jobs? All they do is lie on their backs. Shit's fine when they tell Sin she can't hold Jett's attention and she's deliberately getting pregnant to tighten her grip on him. When we all fuckin' know, it's Jett who keeps knocking Sin up. They mimic Vivie's accent and disrespect her right to her face, thinking that because she is half-French, she won't understand their sarcasm.

"When Ali-kat is told that she better start slimming because Blaze will be put off by her muscles. And ask Ali if she's ever had a spa day because she certainly needs it before the novelty wears off and Blaze wanders. How about when Lindsey's reconstructive surgery fails as she ages, and they show her pictures of surgery gone bad? Or how about our daughter,

Drake, who heard two of them discussing what a stud you were in bed? Think Jodie wants to hear how long and thick your cock is? Or that you keep pace like a jackhammer? Think Jodie wanted to listen to how you love to deep-throat a woman?" Phoe spat, and Drake paled as he glanced at Jodie and saw the truth on her face.

"You walked right over the fact that two whores nearly killed Silvie and her daughter, Drake. They nearly killed an old lady and a princess, but that's okay because your single men fuck them? What value is placed on old ladies and children?" Lindsey spoke up with clear anger in her voice.

"We've all voiced our opinions in private to our husbands, and none of you took them seriously. Because getting a brother's cock sucked by a whore was more important. So be it. We'll remember this. Calamity, I am sorry your celebration ended in such a way, and I promise us old ladies will make it up to you. But for now, let's leave the assholes who value a whore's cunt more than their wife's!" Phoe snarled.

"It's okay, don't worry about it," I said as I felt a clear divide in the room. Old ladies were forcing a stand, and they'd only done this once before. Rosie shuffled by my side and then turned and offered me congrats in her sweet voice before leaving the clubhouse with Serenity, Aurora, Victoria, and Jodie on her heels. Artemis gave a decisive nod at an unspoken message from Phoe. One by one, the old ladies removed themselves from where they were sitting and followed the princesses out. Fuck, what a clusterfuck.

To Drake's surprise, the whores immediately moved in on the single men, and I saw that one action drive the memo home. The old ladies and princesses were disrespected in Rage, and he'd allowed it. The fact the skanks didn't look remotely bothered by the scene spoke volumes to those who had an old lady.

"Sin will never forgive me. First for knocking her up, and now this shit," Jett moaned morosely.

I slapped a hand on his shoulder. "You're gonna have to get on your knees, brother," I replied, and Jett nodded.

"What the fuck do you think you are doing?" Axel bellowed, and we turned to see him facing the skanks as brothers slipped themselves free of them. Even the single brother understood how bad this shit was. And they adored the old ladies. They wouldn't want to place a blow job over one of them.

"Celebrating." Kim beamed at him.

"Take your STD laden skank pussies out of here. I can't get my head around this clusterfuck!" Axel boomed, sending Drake the filthiest look in his arsenal.

Half of us blanched, me included. Drake stared at Axel before turning to Gunner and Apache.

"Get those whores off Rage. We're having church in thirty minutes. Prospects and candidates as well. This is being resolved tonight. Calamity, we'll have a cookout at the weekend," Drake promised.

I smothered a laugh. As per usual, nothing went right for me!

Rosie.

We'd all met up in the Reading Nook. The old
ladies were wildly furious at the stinking attitude of
the skanks and brothers. I wondered if I'd put my foot
in it, but then, listening to the comments, I knew I
hadn't. This fierce confrontation had been building,
and Calamity and I had merely been the catalyst. My
mind drifted to him, so familiar and yet so different.
Calamity had matured over the years, and it showed.
He was still only young, but he held the maturity of a
man twice his age.

Calamity never discussed his history with me. I
knew of his arrival in Rage and how underweight and
abused he'd been. He never once spoke of family or
his past and refused to answer any name besides
Calamity. I had no idea where he hailed from. There
was no discernible accent or anything else to let me
know his home state. There was a sense that Calamity
was from South Dakota, but he didn't confirm it.

Calamity's revelations blew me away tonight. And
I'd witnessed the truth shining in his eyes. He hadn't
touched those skanks, nor had he screwed another
woman. Holy hell, his balls must be the purest blue
going. I was too used to bikers. They fucked when
and where they wished and didn't give a shit who
noticed. At one point, a few times, I had even caught
them having sex in the rec room or at a cookout. I'd

often scurried away, embarrassed for the women with so little pride they'd commit the act of sex out in the open. But scouring my brain, I'd never seen Calamity doing that.

I was struggling with the truth that Calamity had held back for nearly four years waiting for me. Slowly, I began to accept it. My heart cracked with what I knew was love. Calamity had never pushed himself on me. He was often shy and unassuming, but tonight I'd heard a man who knew what he wanted and intended to claim it.

"Your father will shit a brick," a soft voice spoke next to me, and I jumped. Penny's kind eyes observed me with knowledge and awareness of my feelings.

"I love him," I whispered.

"Not surprised, baby girl," she responded, raising a hand to stroke my hair. "That boy is the epitome of everything good and honourable. Calamity will break his neck to make you happy and strive to give you anything you need and want."

"Calam is a great guy," I said fiercely, and Penny nodded.

"But that won't change the fact Texas will shit a brick. You're his baby girl, and he wants much better than a biker for you. Texas has never made bones about that, Rosie. And the entire club knows princesses are off-limits. Calamity has a mountain to scale, but I don't doubt he would walk through fire for you."

"Think Dad will turn against him?" I asked in a small voice.

"I believe Texas will rant and rave for a while before recognising this is what you want and that you truly love each other. All Texas wants is for you to be happy. He'll eventually come around. Probably after putting his foot in his mouth several times. Just make sure he pays through the nose when you forgive him." Penny winked, and I began laughing.

I loved this woman!

Chapter Three.

Calamity

I was riding home when something moved on the roadside. I'd spent the day with Micah, now Fanatic, working out a new design for a matching bike and car we were designing for auction. We'd both promised Phoe something special, and we'd had our heads together all day fine-tuning out designs. The faint movement nearly passed me, but it caught my attention, and I pulled over.

Getting off the Harley, my pride and joy, which I looked after like my own child, I noticed the action again and bent down. A hiss of disgust and worry left my mouth when I saw a wounded dog lying in the dirt. A quick glance informed me this poor animal was severely injured and nearly dying. Quickly, I shrugged off my riding jacket and wrapped the canine up before climbing back on the motorbike. Carefully keeping the dog tight, I throttled the bike and headed to where I knew I could get help.

Thirty minutes later, I arrived at the clinic Rosie worked at. I'd been by plenty of times but never stopped to check it out. Quickly getting off the Harley, I hurried inside and met several people sitting and waiting and a stone-faced receptionist.

"Need Rosie. Is she in?" I gasped, hurrying over.

"Rosie?" she asked, looking down her nose.

Her badge said, Chelsea.

"Dr Rosie Craven. Rosie's a vet here. Need her urgently," I explained.

"Do you have an appointment?"

"Just said I have to see her. Found this dog badly wounded at the side of the road, and it needs help. Think it's dying," I responded quickly. "Look, get Rosie."

"Take a seat," Chelsea stated, eyeing me, and I saw the dismissal in her eyes. This poor pup would be dead before I got aid.

"Rosie!" I bellowed.

"Sit down before I phone law enforcement!" Chelsea snapped.

"Rosie!" I roared again and heard doors opening in the corridor behind the desk.

A guy stuck out his head, frowning.

"What's going on?" he inquired.

"I need to see Rosie Craven right now!" I demanded.

"Call the police," the guy ordered, and the receptionist picked up the phone.

"Calamity?" Rosie asked, appearing next to the asshole.

"Rosie, I was riding back from Hellfire and found this pup in the road. It's hurt. Can you help?"

"Bring him through," Rosie said, and I followed her, glaring at the secretary and the man. Rosie unlocked a door with her name on it, and I rushed to the table and placed the dog on it. Rosie opened my jacket, gasped, and then hurried into action.

"Winnie!" Rosie called, and a woman stormed in.

"What do we have, Doc?" Winnie asked, cleansing her hands. Rosie began rattling commands as she carefully started checking the animal over.

"Calamity, wait outside," Rosie spoke as she concentrated on the wounded animal.

"Don't let him die, Rosie," I begged.

"Do my best, Calam; please leave so I can concentrate," Rosie replied, her soft eyes meeting mine.

Upset, I nodded and left. Pent up with worry and frustration, I paced the waiting room, keeping a sharp watch on the corridor. The receptionist kept an eye on me as minutes ticked by. Every so often, Chelsea glanced towards the parking lot and finally, a smug smile was sent my way. To claim it was a surprise was a lie when two uniforms entered.

"Bobby, Dan," I greeted, and they said hello.

While Dan spoke to the stuck-up bitch, Bobby came over.

"What's going on? We got a call you were being aggressive and making threats," Bobby announced.

"Bullshit," I announced, loud enough for the secretary to flinch. "Guessing the lying cunt doesn't realise Hawthorne organises security here. Give Max a call. I'm betting Max has already pulled it. That means, bitch, everything I did was recorded, so you just filed a false report. What's the penalty for that nowadays?" I idly asked Bobby, whose lips twitched.

The receptionist flinched as I bared my teeth.

"Tell me what happened, Calamity," Bobby stated.

I quickly explained while keeping my eye on the corridor for any sign of Rosie. The pup had been so badly wounded it was a miracle I'd got it here alive.

"And the dog, Calamity?" Bobby asked.

"To be honest, I don't know. Appeared to have been in a fight, but the wounds could easily have been caused by a car. Ain't no vet, but the poor thing was in a terrible state. I'm praying Rosie can save him," I replied.

"Ma'am, would you like to amend your statement before RCPD pulls the footage and checks it? Making a false complaint will rebound on you," I overheard Dan say sternly.

The receptionist stuttered, and Chelsea glanced over her shoulder at the guy who had egged her on. Surprise, he was nowhere to be found. Sullenly, Chelsea admitted she might have been frightened by my cut and exaggerated. Dan and Bobby began giving her a severe telling-off, ignoring the gossiping onlookers. When they finished, Chelsea's face was redder than a tomato.

"Calamity."

I turned, strode over to Rosie, and rested my hands on her shoulders.

"How is he?" I asked.

Rosie wiped a tear away, and my heart sank.

"Alive, but in a bad state. I'm glad you called Bobby and Dan. This needs reporting," Rosie said, and I felt a shudder run through her body. I yanked Rosie in close and held her tightly for a few seconds, and she relaxed before she gathered her strength.

"What's up, Rosie?" Bobby asked.

"The dog, he'd been in a fight. I recognise the wounds. Someone is running a fighting ring," Rosie whispered. And bam. Rosie dropped a bomb on us. Disgust curled my lip as my eyes narrowed. Bobby and Dan wore mirroring expressions of hatred.

"My nurse, Winnie, is taking pictures. The poor thing has been torn to pieces and clearly dumped for dead. Will you inform Ramirez or Nando? We require one of them on this," Rosie urged.

"Gather all the evidence we need. Honey, I'll pop in tomorrow and collect it. Ramirez is on a case, but I think Nando freed some time. Let me put in a call, but I'll make sure it's someone you're familiar with. Is that okay?" Bobby asked gently.

My lip curled at Bobby calling Rosie honey, and I saw mischief in his eyes. I sent Bobby a warning glance, which made him chuckle.

"Nando is fine. Winnie and I will collect everything you need," Rosie said.

"And I'll let Nando know where I found the dog. There may have been others dumped there, and I didn't see them," I replied, and Rosie butted in.

"We have to check Calamity. If there are any more alive, we must hurry!" The urgency on Rosie's face convinced me before even her words did.

"Fine, we'll use your car. Bobby, if we find anything else, we'll phone. Chelsea, please cancel my last two appointments, as this is an emergency."

The receptionist shot Rosie a dark stare but nodded.

Bobby regained my attention. "Calamity, call me, and I'll pass the info on to the detective, who'll take charge," Bobby replied.

Rosie hurried away as I sent a puzzled look after her. She returned a few minutes later carrying a medical bag. In approval, I responded to Rosie's alertness and followed her to the car. Luckily for me, Rosie drove an SUV, which would make moving any injured dogs easier. I leapt into the passenger side, noting Rosie's startled expression.

"You don't want to drive?" Rosie demanded as she climbed in and started the engine. Rosie yanked her seatbelt into place and roared out of the parking lot.

"No, I'm secure enough in my manhood, baby, that you can drive," I teased, and Rosie rolled her eyes. Calmly, I directed Rosie to where I'd found the dog, and thirty minutes later, we pulled over.

"Poor thing was there," I said, pointing to the slope I had seen the canine on. Rosie scrambled down the sides, and I followed with a muffled curse.

"Oh God," Rosie exclaimed in a broken cry and turned and jammed into my chest. My arms rose automatically around her as my horrified sight took in the graveyard of over a dozen dumped dogs.

"Rosie, we need to check if there's any living. Stay here, baby," I said, swallowing bile. Rosie shook her head and gathered herself together, and we started checking each dog. It wasn't until we reached the back we found two alive. Rosie began working straight away while I called Bobby. We'd counted as we had looked for signs of life. Twenty-three dogs had been dumped here. All showing wounds from dogfighting.

With tears, Rosie picked up one of those alive while I gathered the second. We carried them to the car as soon as Rosie felt they could be moved. The sorrow and pain in Rosie's face cut deep, and I longed to reassure her, but looking at the scale of death around us, it was impossible. I hated cruelty, but to force dogs to fight and then leave them dumped in a ditch on the roadside was unspeakable.

"Go get them out of here. Baby, I'll wait for Bobby," I said. Rosie offered a doubtful gaze, and I kissed her head. "They're more important. Come and collect me if I'm not at the clinic by the time you've finished. But go, honey, save those poor pups."

Rosie nodded and leapt into the SUV, and the wheels skidded as she completed a turn and sped off. Upset, I dragged my phone out and called Drake, letting him know where I was and what I'd found. I told Drake that Rosie had two alive still and was rushing them to the vets she worked at. Drake said to stay put and that somebody would meet me. Fair enough.

Rosie

Without concern, I rushed into the clinic carrying the worst injured of the dogs. Brett met me as I entered, a quizzical expression on his face. I dumped the dog in his arms and ran back for the second.

"Rosie, what is this? We are not a charity!" Brett exclaimed on my return.

I sent Brett a menacing stare.

"They are wounded and victims of a fighting ring. One would think decency alone would make you want to help," I snapped.

"Rosie, it would be kinder to euthanise them," Brett sneered.

Winnie appeared, and I handed over my dog, and she raced away, and I snatched the one from Brett's arms.

"Wonder what the RCPD would say when I tell them you tried to get rid of evidence," I retorted and headed to my room.

Winnie and I bust our asses for the next three hours, trying to save both dogs. It was a testament to our skills that we stabilised them. Wearily placing them inside cages, I checked the first one Calamity had brought me and saw he was looking far better. A beep made me look down, and I opened a text from Calamity stating he was heading to the clinic and to stay there. Tiredly, I sent an okay back and a quick message informing Calamity all animals were alive. Calamity responded with two heart emojis and three thumbs up, making me smile.

"Who's that?" Brett demanded, attempting to peer over my shoulder.

Defensively, I moved swiftly away. I didn't like Brett's smarmy, cringeworthy attempts at flirting. There was something decidedly strange with Brett, and he wouldn't accept no for an answer.

"Private is what that is," I replied lightly, unwilling to argue.

"That biker?" Brett demanded, almost spitting the last word.

"What if it is? My life is nothing to do with you," I said as I walked to my room and began washing and sterilising everything.

"You don't need to date a dirty biker if I am here, Rosie. Look, I know you're playing hard to get, but lowering yourself to that scum is unnecessary."

Furious, I spun on Brett.

"You've no idea who I am, do you? I'm a biker's daughter. My father is an officer in Rage MC, and you stand there and spit on bikers? I suggest you leave Brett because you are really insulting me now, and I'm taking offence," I demanded with a vicious swipe at the table.

"Rosie, you've risen above that existence. And I respect that. Do not lower yourself by dating a biker and going back to that kind of life," Brett spoke condescendingly.

"I beg your pardon!" I exclaimed, outraged. "Escaped that life? Lower myself? I'm a Rage princess. That fact has never changed and never will. Whatever image you built up of me is badly warped. I am proud of Rage, my dad, and my role in the MC. Who the hell do you think you're talking to?" I demanded, beyond furious now.

Brett stepped forward, and sexual desire and malice shone in his eyes.

"So you're just another dirty whore!" Brett cried and reached out to grab my arms.

I struggled to get free as Brett used his body to pin me to the counters. Brett's mouth descended on mine, and I twisted my head.

"Get your fuckin' hands off her!" Calamity bellowed, and Brett let go and turned.

Calamity barrelled across the room and dragged me behind him.

"Dude, bitch wanted it. She was begging me for some action. Rosie's just another dirty whore," Brett sneered as he looked Calamity up and down.

I didn't see Calamity move, but Brett reeled back, holding his nose, and I realised Calamity had punched him.

"You ever touch Rosie again without her permission and worse will follow," Calamity promised, murder in his eyes.

"Bastard, I'll have you arrested," Brett snarled as he tried to stem the nosebleed.

"And so will I! You attacked me! I'll be speaking to Doctor Steiner about this!" I yelled. Brett scoffed at the mention of the owner of the vets, which was his uncle. The practise employed four vets; the fourth was Doctor Steiner's wife, who used her own maiden name to practise. Janine Jones and Doctor Steiner both owned the clinic.

"Go ahead," Brett sneered. "See what my aunt and uncle do. They won't side with a dirty whore of a biker's daughter."

"Well, if they don't discipline you, I'll take private action because your attack was on camera!" I retorted, and Brett paled a little.

"Get the fuck out of here," Calamity warned, and Brett scurried away.

"Thanks," I said with a loud sigh.

"Rosie, I'll call Hawthorne," Calamity stated as his eyes checked me.

"Fine," I replied, exhausted.

As we left, I ran up the bill for the care of the three dogs and then paid on my card. I would not allow Brett any leverage. And Brett would spill the beans to Janine and Ralph before I could blink. Now I could prove the dog's medical care had been sorted.

"Fancy dinner?" Calamity asked.

"I'd love to, but I'm so tired." I yawned, and Calamity smiled.

"Come on. I know exactly what you need. Are you okay to drive, or shall I?" Calamity urged.

"No, I can drive. Not that tired."

"Good, follow me." Calamity winked as I shut the lights off and locked the doors. I followed Calamity to my favourite eating place in Rapid City. A family-run Mexican restaurant where the food was handmade and authentic. Calamity knew me too well. The owner smiled as he ushered us to a private table, where I instantly relaxed as the spicy smells washed over me.

"The usual?" Calamity grinned.

"Yup." I sighed happily.

"A sharing nacho starter followed by two lots of chicken enchiladas, with quesadilla and accompaniments and chicken rice, please. For dessert, two chocolate churros with vanilla bean ice cream. We'll take two cokes as well," Calamity placed the order as soon as the waitress came over.

"Now tell me about that asshole. Has he touched you before?" Calamity demanded.

I glanced at him. The intent expression I observed on his face ensured I knew Calamity wouldn't let this go until he had answers.

"No. Brett's made verbal suggestions and crude comments but never gone so far as to touch me. I've threatened him with all sorts of action, and usually, Brett backs off. Tonight, he wouldn't have it. Something about you triggered him," I said honestly.

Calamity leaned forward.

"You'll be safe, Rosie. Trust me," he swore.

"Don't you already know, Calam? Honey, I trust you to the moon and back."

Calamity smiled smugly, and I rolled my eyes.

"Dr Craven, can you come to my office, please," Dr

Janine Jones asked towards the end of my shift the next day.

Winnie and I exchanged glances. Janine was never formal.

"Sure, just let me wash my hands, and I'll be there," I replied, and Janine offered a stiff nod.

As I left my workspace and walked to Janine's, I passed Brett, who presented a smug smile. I grinned at the two black eyes and snorted, making Brett glower before I knocked and entered Janine's room. Janine glared as I took a chair, folded my hands neatly, and gazed patiently at her. I knew exactly what this was about, but I intended to keep my cool. Because I doubted Janine had all the facts.

"Well, Dr Craven, let's start by saying how happy I've been with your work until now. You're dedicated, loyal, caring, and have a high success rate. You've been an exemplary employee," Janine said.

"Thank you."

"Until yesterday. While I did not know you had links to an MC, you kept your personal and professional life separate. It didn't matter until it affected your performance. For you to freely treat a dog that a member of an MC had illegally fought and then two further victims is despicable. And not a standard I'd expect of an employee. Needless to say, you treating them without charging the customer, and intending to return them to the brute, speaks of a lack of morals I don't wish to employ.

"Dr Craven, you are quite lucky that I haven't called the police for your friend attacking my nephew when he objected to the dogs being used to fight. However, those victims won't be leaving this clinic. Brett has suffered a facial injury through the uncalled-for assault by your companion. And allowing such behaviour to continue is unacceptable, and I will inform the police of the three animals in our care. On the grounds of offering free treatment for illegal activities, I have no recourse but to terminate your employment." Janine sat back and stared sternly.

I smiled.

"So, no explanation needed from me?" I inquired.

Janine sneered. "No, you're as corrupt as the men you surround yourself with. Dr Craven, I won't have those standards here," she responded.

Agreeably, I nodded and pulled out my phone. Janine watched, confused, as I dialled a number.

"Can I speak to Detective Hernando Hawthorne, please?" I asked, and Janine frowned. Quietly, I placed the call on the loudspeaker.

"Hello?" a deep voice urged.

"Nando, it's Rosie," I said.

"Hi Rosie, how's things? Please tell me you've not had another dog brought in?"

"No, Nando, nothing like that. But I was wondering if you had any leads? I know Calamity and I only found those dogs yesterday, but they're innocents, Nando, and I hate the thought of more being hurt."

"Rosie, I'm sorry, chick. I appreciate how hard it must be for you in your job. When Calamity discovered the first one, I'd hoped with Bobby's report that it would be a one-off. When you and Calamity retraced his steps and found the graveyard, I knew we had a big problem. Rosie, I've spoken to the chief.

"He is as concerned as you and Calamity are. Chief asked me to ask Rage to keep their ears to the ground for any hints of dog fighting, and I've already contacted Hawthorne's. The chief wants you to phone all other vets in the area and see if they've had any victims brought in. And the chief said for you to be the contact for them, which leaves my partner and me open to investigate," Nando said.

Janine's eyebrows flew up into her hairline.

"Justin Goldberg?" I quizzed, and Nando expressed an affirmative.

"Got to say, pretty damned good of your clinic to treat those poor animals for free," Nando said.

"Oh, they didn't. Because they don't give free care for victims of dog fighting, so I paid," I responded, dug into my bag, and slid the receipt across to Janine.

Her mouth pursed.

"Oh honey, look, that had to cost a whack. Let me do a whip round at the PD, and we'll give you some help. None of us wants to see dogs abused like that," Nando expressed in concern.

"That's not needed, Nando," I replied, smiling.

"But it is. You stay safe, and give my respects to your dad and the club. Speak soon. And Rosie, if you discover any information, don't go off half-cocked. Know you love animals, but your health and safety mean more to us," Nando warned.

"Okay, see you at the cookout Saturday," I teased, and Nando groaned.

"Send me a text. Lord knows which kid's birthday it is this time!"

I laughed, cut the phone, and stared straight at Janine.

"From the moment my time was used to the very last bandage, everything is itemised. I paid for everything, including billing my hours," I told Janine firmly.

"I don't understand," Janine said, shaking her head.

"No, because you believed your lying nephew. Neither Calamity nor my father's club are involved in this. Calamity called law enforcement as soon as he realised what he had in his hands, an illegal fighting ring. He spoke to RCPD yesterday and informed them he and I would investigate where Calamity came upon the first dog. With permission from the police, we did just that and discovered more bodies and two barely alive pups. I brought them back, and Brett refused to work on them. Winnie is a witness to that. I worked on both and saved their lives.

"Later that evening, Brett entered my office and made several accusations about not needing to date a biker. Who and when I date has nothing to do with Brett. When Brett discovered my father was a biker, he sexually assaulted me. Calamity interrupted him and punched him in my defence. Now I hadn't been planning to press charges, but with all Brett's lies running around, I have little choice," I said.

"You're lying to get out of your friend's assault,"

Janine cried angrily.

I picked up the phone again and dialled.

"Hi Max, it's Rosie. Can you send the footage, please?"

"On its way. We're on standby should you need help," Max replied.

I thanked him, heard a ping, and then played the video, starting when Brett entered my office. Janine went pale as she realised there was only one way this could be construed and that I'd told the truth.

"What do you want?" Janine whispered.

Well, now, what an interesting question.

Chapter Four.

Rosie

"Janine, I don't want anything, just to do my job and go home. Brett's lies are because he got caught sexually assaulting a colleague. And it isn't the first time. There are other witnesses to Brett's fumbled attempts. And enough is enough. I hadn't brought this to your attention because it was my word against Brett's. But after the pack of rubbish Brett's told you today, I'm informing you I'll no longer work in a hostile atmosphere. As of now, I'm putting in an official grievance against Brett for his actions and slanderous allegations. And please remember that even this office is recorded," I stated.

"Doctor Steiner and I will have a discussion with Brett," Janine said, and I shook my head.

"That's not good enough. Janine, I'm placing a complaint. And I want it to be properly investigated and appropriate action taken. Brett has created and now enforced a hostile working atmosphere for me here. Honestly, I feel I can't work here much longer, and I am giving you notice I will be looking for another job. Because your idea of having a chat with Brett isn't the correct procedure when someone is accused of sexual misconduct. I shall contact a lawyer, and we'll see what happens. In the meantime, I expect to do my job without interference or penalties," I responded, rising from my seat.

Janine looked mulish and disgruntled, but that wasn't my fault.

As I left the room, I saw Brett lurking and looking smug.

"Poor play because everything you did was on camera, and now the practise faces a lawsuit," I said.

Brett's face fell, and he dashed into his aunt's office. Annoyed, I headed to mine and called the club's lawyer.

After listening to his advice, I planned for the victims of dogfighting to be moved to a different vet. Then I wrote out my notice, explaining why I was leaving. My lawyer was already drawing up a lawsuit. An hour after the meeting with Janine, my lawyer okayed the resignation letter. I walked back into Janine's office, handed it to her, and informed Janine my lawyer would soon be in touch.

As I left, I saw Brett lurking and glowering again as I collected my belongings and exited the clinic. I'd been there a year and was upset at having to leave. Would I be able to get another job, or would the

Steiner's attempt to blacklist me?

Calamity

I was surprised to see Rosie heading to her car carrying a box. I pulled up and jumped off my Harley.

"What's going on?" I demanded, making Rosie jump. A sheepish smile crossed my lips but faded when I took in Rosie's pallor.

"Rosie?"

"Calam, follow me home, and I'll explain."

"Have those fuckers fired you?" I exclaimed, turning on my heel.

"Calamity, no!" Rosie cried, and she grabbed my arm.

"Then what?" I growled, glaring at the building.

"Come to my house, and we'll talk. Please, Calam, I just want to leave," Rosie muttered. Swiftly, I considered my options for a few moments before finally nodding and climbing on my Harley. Funny enough, I'd never been to Rosie's home, although I knew where she lived. Rosie owned several acres of land outside the city with a farmhouse. I followed, worrying that Rosie was upset and had been fired because I punched that motherfucker that dared touch her. When Rosie parked, I leapt off my bike as she struggled to pick up the heavy box.

"Here, babe, I'll carry it," I said and took it. Moments later, I dropped it as I scurried backwards.

"What the fuck is that?" I shrieked, not ashamed of the high girlish tone. Rosie had opened the front door, and a fucking overgrown Labrador and Cujo's twin brother bounded out.

"Rosie, get away now!" I ordered as she began laughing as the massive canines headed towards me. Hell, I was about to be eaten alive.

"Layla, Henrik, sit," Rosie cried, and I swear to God she was crying with laughter.

The two dogs sat, and I eyed them warily.

"Rosie," I drawled slowly as Cujo's twin licked his chops.

"Calamity, hold out a hand," Rosie said, approaching.

Fear rose as Cujo twisted and stared. Moments later, Cujo flopped on his back, and Rosie bent and gave him a tummy rub. His tail wagged so hard he created little dust storms. Meanwhile, the Labrador on steroids watched me with his head tilted to one side.

"Calamity, meet Layla. She is a Great Pyrenees. She's two years old, and I've had her since she was a puppy."

I eyed Layla, who put a paw out and gazed at me with soft eyes. Layla was a beautiful creature, with a thick creamy white coat and gentle brown eyes, and she stood about two and a half feet high. Gingerly, I took the paw, shook it, and then staggered back as Layla rose on her hind legs and landed her front paws on my shoulder. Layla buried her head in my neck and licked before getting down.

"Layla likes you. Those were doggie kisses. She

doesn't even do that for Dad." Rosie giggled.

Meanwhile, Cujo was tired of having his belly rubbed and was now on all fours, staring.

"This is Henrik. He is a Bernese Mountain dog. I've had Henrik for a year, and he's two years old. He got too big for his previous owner, who locked Henrik in a shed and left him to starve."

Anger crossed my face. I hated cruelty to animals; that was one of my pet peeves. Henrik sat and held up a paw. I took it carefully, and Henrik tilted his head before lying down and showing me his stomach. At Rosie's encouraging nod, I gave Henrik a vigorous rub, and Henrik let out a bark of happiness.

He was beautifully marked with tan colouring on his legs and tufts on his cheeks and either side of his chest. Henrik had four white paws and a white chest, while the rest of him was a thick black coat. His nose and mouth were white, with a trail leading up between his eyes. Henrik was two and a half feet high, slightly smaller than Layla.

Rosie whistled, both bounded towards her, and she opened a gate in the fence. I finally took a long look around.

We had turned off the main street and driven about half a mile down a private road, which led to an open area where we'd parked. The house stood in the middle, with fences leading down to the tree line and continuing around the trees. I imagined Rosie's entire acreage was fenced in, keeping it safe for the dogs to roam. The home was a beautiful old farmhouse with a wraparound porch and a matching first-floor balcony.

The second floor had balconies placed in front of French doors. Each window and set of doors had shutters painted sky blue, with the windows having flower boxes. The red tiles on the roof shone in the sun, and the entire image was of a pretty postcard farmhouse, complete with porch swings and rocking chairs.

"Stunning," I said to Rosie and nodded towards the house.

"Yeah, it needed some serious renovation, but the bones were there when I moved in. Uncle Apache and Rock did the repairs and helped me recreate her beauty."

"Bet they fenced in the acreage, too?"

"Yes. That cost a whack, but the animals can run freely, and I don't have to worry about them getting lost or finding the main road. Are you coming in?"

"Anymore Cujo's waiting?" I teased, and Rosie looked mischievous but shook her head.

Rosie's look warned me, but nothing prepared me for what I saw next. I followed Rosie into a hallway and through a door leading into a living room that ran the length of the house. A massive ball of grey fluff with a white nose rose from an armchair, and I gazed in horror. The disgusted stare from the regal face almost made me laugh.

"What the hell is that?" I asked, putting the box down as Rosie gathered the furball in her arms. The damn thing was nearly as tall as her.

"This one is Merlin, and he's a Maine Coon. And this is Arthur, and he's a Norwegian Forrest cat,"

Rosie declared and pointed as a ginger, tawny and tabby-coloured feline rose. Arthur wasn't as big as Merlin but was still a handful. Arthur wound himself around my legs, and I picked him up as he purred loudly.

"Christ, he's a weight," I gasped.

"Twelve pounds, and he's a beautiful, healthy kitty," Rosie replied, making kissy noises.

I laughed as Arthur tilted his head towards her. This one was a mommy's boy.

"Motherfucker in the house. Pay the piper, bastard," came a screech that made me jump.

Shocked, I looked around while Rosie started scolding someone unseen.

"Nope, I'm telling, pay me asshole," the scream came again.

I finally recognised it as a bird and began looking for a parrot. Astonished, I saw a black raven stick its head out of a curtain.

"Mom, Peter is cursing," a second voice said, and I frowned. Where were the missing parrots?

"Shut up, Precious," the caw returned, and there was a definite raspberry.

"Mind your manners," the second voice retorted, and I smiled. This was quite funny.

"Mind the asshole intruder in Rosie's bedroom. Tell Texas," the first screeched.

"I'm going to cap your ass," the second replied, and I began laughing.

"I don't see them, Rosie; where are the parrots?" I urged.

76

Rosie grinned and nodded at the black raven.

"He talks?" I asked, astounded.

"They both do. Ravens can talk. If you're patient, they can learn quite a vocabulary. Unfortunately, Dad has spent a bit too much time with Peter. But I have Precious. Come here, darling girl," Rosie coaxed as she placed Merlin on the ground. A head poked out from the curtains and ducked shyly back. After a couple of minutes of coaxing, I stared at a beautiful, glossy white bird.

"What is she?"

"A white raven. They are very rare and extremely clever. Here, put your arm out," Rosie ordered, and I obeyed cautiously.

Precious twitched and rubbed her beak against Rosie as Rosie encouraged her onto me. Slowly and warily, Precious stepped across, and I was awestruck as she sidestepped her way to my shoulder. Precious gave me a quick cheek rub and then flew back to her safe place behind the curtain.

"Precious is shy, but once she gets used to you, prepare to dish the love," Rosie declared as Peter cussed me out.

"Peter, no treat," Rosie said, and the black raven made a strangling noise. Peter turned his head and eyed me balefully.

"Sleep with your eyes open, fucker," he warned, and I burst into laughter again.

"Anything else I need to know about?"

"I've got a few more pets," Rosie admitted.

Next, I met Empress, the most beautiful black and

grey Persian I'd ever seen. And the smallest, Rosie said, her breed was a Teacup Persian. Empress literally would fit into a teacup. And like an empress, she rode around on Merlin, which had me in stitches as she sat regally between his ears. Then there was Wolfie, one of the ugliest cats I'd come across. Rosie explained he was called a Lykoi, as he resembled a werewolf. Wolfie was skinny with sparse, thin fur, but shit, his facial markings made him look like a feline werewolf.

Then there was Jester, a beautiful white artic fox who wound his way around your legs much like a cat. Jester loved to be picked up and have his belly rubbed. And when you put him down before he was satisfied, Jester nipped your ankles. Rosie had a hedgehog named Harold and a tortoise called Terence. Finally, to my shock, there was a muntjac deer, Dawn, that Rosie had hand raised after finding her wounded as a baby.

"You've got a right zoo going on," I teased Rosie, who shrugged as she bent and gave Terence a tomato. Anyone who says tortoises are slow are lying bastards. That fucker flew across the kitchen to grab his prize. I was bemused as all the animals crowded into Rosie's large kitchen for a treat. Even Dawn came for hers, and I fed it to her, feeling spellbound. I felt a thud on my shoe and saw Terence standing there.

"What the fuck?" I asked as I watched Terence waddle backwards and then speed towards me again and, at the last minute, draw his head back in, and his shell hit my boot.

"Don't ask me. Terrence's always done that, ever since I was little. Dad got him for me as a baby, and Terence just thumps people. Watch out if you're barefoot because he hurts. We've also taught him to play soccer, and Terence has an assault course Dad and I built. Greg and Daisy love him to bits," Rosie explained as Terence banged into me again. Harold waddled past me as Terence stepped back, and with a slight jump in the air, Harold curled into a ball and rolled away.

"This is chaos," I gasped, laughing hard.

Empress stared regally from between Merlin's ears while Peter regaled me with every curse word he'd had to have learned from Texas. Including a few I recognised from Sin, twatwaffle, numpty, and several more. Dawn, meanwhile, was head-butting me for another treat, and Jester was attempting to climb my jeans for a fuss.

"Yeah, but they are so loveable," Rosie added. She opened the back door, which was a handy stable design, and I saw the cutest little goat ever.

"There you are, Fanny," Rosie said.

"Oh my God, that's so cute!" I exclaimed. It was pure white with black socks and a black star on her head. The goat stared at me in horror, stiffened, and then fell over.

"Rosie!" I yelled and dashed forward, kneeling at the poor thing's feet. It was completely stiff, and I frantically tried searching for a heartbeat.

To my surprise, Rosie laughed hard at my actions,

and I glared.

"Rosie, come and help. Please, I didn't mean to kill her!" I gasped.

"Calam, Fanny's a Myotonic Goat, a Tennessee Fainting Goat. Any loud noise makes her faint and fall over," Rosie explained through her chuckles.

"What the fuck, Rosie!" I roared as Fanny got to her feet.

With a sharp bleat, Fanny stiffened and fell on her other side. Oh God, I was making this poor creature pass out.

"What do I do?" I whispered, desperate not to make Fanny faint again.

"Just keep loud noises to a minimum. Although Peter does like to set her off," Rosie said with a scowl.

I'd never felt so guilty as brown eyes blinked, and slowly Fanny climbed to her feet. I had a carrot in my hand, and Fanny snatched it from me and began nibbling daintily. A low chuckle escaped as Fanny regarded me with a baleful gaze.

"Is this all the menagerie?" I asked Rosie.

"Yes, Fanny has got Dad and everyone else who visited. Dad tried to give her mouth-to-mouth. It was freaking hysterical." Rosie giggled. Dawn nudged at Fanny to share her carrot, and Fanny offered her a dirty look before taking off.

"That's why you require all this land? So, the animals can roam freely and safely," I said, sitting on my haunches. Jester had clearly decided that I was his person as he crawled into my lap while Henrik slumped next to me on the floor.

"Yup, the dogs need a large area to run, and so do Dawn and Fanny. Harold rarely goes further than the flower beds, but Jester sometimes takes off on a sprint."

A thud landed on my hip as Terence made his presence known. Fuck, that would leave a bruise.

"So, what happened at work?" I asked as Rosie switched the kettle on.

The animals had scattered, going back to doing whatever they were before.

Rosie quickly explained while my temper moved. I let out a loud exclamation at one point, and Fanny wheezed and fell over. Guilt swamped my anger as I picked up the tiny goat and stroked her until she woke up. I was completely furious with how this Janine had treated Rosie and longed to do nothing more than go tearing after her. But Rosie played it smart, and I had to follow her lead. There was another matter we needed to discuss urgently.

"How do we tell your father?" I asked Rosie, and she cocked her head, confused.

"About Brett? Oh, leave that to me," Rosie replied.

"No, babe, about us. You know why I am here. Rosie, you know why I hung around. You're mine, and I'm laying claim to you. Now I'm a full brother; there shouldn't be any impediments. I work as well as attend college. Not as clever as you, but I will get my qualifications in design. Rosie, I couldn't claim you as a prospect. I wasn't good enough. Fuck, I'm still not enough, but I love you and have for years," I said honestly. Rosie's eyes melted, and she came and sat next to me.

"I love you too, Calam, and I understand why you had to wait all these years. Dad would never have allowed me to date a prospect," Rosie replied.

I leaned forward, cupped the back of her head, and kissed her lips. They tasted as I imagined, sweet and plump. My body lit on fire as heat flooded my veins at the first taste of Rosie I'd properly had. Her lips parted between mine, and we both deepened the kiss. I could sense Rosie's arousal, which made my cock as hard as steel. Desperately, I wanted to strip her naked, sink between her legs, and feast. But I needed to court Rosie correctly and honourably.

Before we took that step, I would ask permission from Texas to date Rosie. There was no reason I couldn't. I was a full brother. I had money in the bank and could take care of her. There was no barrier to us being together that I could foresee. Texas and I just needed a man-to-man chat, and as soon as he knew I was serious, we'd have his blessing. The kiss broke off, and I saw the desire in Rosie's eyes.

"We can't until we talk to Texas," I said.

"Shit, you and your honour. Calam, I want you to take me to bed and give me a good pounding," Rosie declared cheekily.

I choked just as Fanny peeked and then fainted.

"Jesus Christ, this goat is going to hate me!" I exclaimed as Rosie broke down into laughter again.

We spent the rest of the day together, me learning how to feed the pets and walking the ground with her.

I spied a piece of land separate from the main grounds and asked Rosie what she plotted to do with it. Shyly, Rosie explained she planned to open a clinic in ten years. She didn't have student loans, thanks to Texas, although she had tried to pay him back. And her grandparents had left enough capital to buy this property, so anything Rosie earned she squirrelled away, intending to establish and run her own vet service one day. It was an idea that stuck in my head.

Despite only being in Rage for four years, I'd earned good money and not spent a cent. I could easily afford to build Rosie a clinic. The question was, how expensive was veterinary equipment? Great quality medical equipment wasn't going to be cheap. I began thinking of ways to get Rosie what she needed sooner rather than later. There wasn't a chance in hell that I wanted Rosie exposed to another Brett, and my stomach twisted at the thought. I would give Rosie everything she desired.

I left Rosie's at ten. We'd played with the animals, and I'd roared with laughter at Peter's foul mouth. There was no denying Texas's influence on the potty-mouthed cheeky raven. Peter's crazy talk brought Precious out time and time again to berate him, but I saw the twinkle in Peter's eye as she did. He was deliberately baiting the shy white raven. I pulled into Rage with a huge grin on my face. I adored all of Rosie's unique and wonderful pets. But I was surprised nobody had ever mentioned them before.

Did no one visit my beautiful girl?

As I stepped into the clubhouse, Texas shot me a look, and Drake whistled. What the fuck? Had they found out my intentions about Rosie already? Drake tilted his head toward church, and I walked towards it, feeling like I was going to the gallows.

"Everything okay?" Texas asked, raking me with a stern gaze.

"Yeah, sure," I replied.

Texas and Drake swapped glances.

"Had a suit here hunting for you. Called you by name, Billy Tomkins," Texas claimed, and I jumped in my seat.

"Hope you told him Billy Tomkins is dead. That he doesn't exist no more," I growled.

"The suit was a lawyer, Calamity. Mentioned that he'd had a PI searching for you, and the trail led here. We didn't deny or confirm you were here. What's going on, Calamity?" Drake demanded.

My past. Had it caught up to me? Why a suit and not local cops? If I were wanted for Mrs Travis's murder, surely it would be the police? Fuck, nothing was simple. I was about to get my chance with Rosie and may have to run. I couldn't take my precious girl on the run with me. Were my fuckin' parents about to screw my life up?

"Nothing Drake, I'll handle it. Did he leave a card?"

"Calamity, brothers do not stand alone. Mac has already investigated this guy. He's genuine. A real lawyer. Now, why is he wanting you?" Drake pried.

"Honestly, I don't know. Billy Tomkins came from

rubbish, was born of trash, and grew up trash. Ain't no reason a lawyer is looking for me except for trouble. If he comes back, tell me. Because I might need to plan," I replied.

Drake didn't like that. His spine straightened, and his shoulders stiffened.

"You speak to me before you make any plans. Is that clear?" Drake snapped.

"Sure, Pres."

"Calamity, no brother takes on shit alone. I mean it. If he comes again, we'll dig into why, but are you certain there's nothing you got to hide?" Texas pushed.

"Yeah," I mumbled. Only the fact I'm crazy in love with your daughter. And the old lady who loved me was discovered dead at the bottom of her stairs. Knowing my parents, they'd try to say I killed her because I fought back against them. Sure, there was nothing Rage needed to know; please note the sarcasm. I rose to my feet. It was time to be alone and devise an exit plan.

The gutting thing was, I knew no idea would include Rosie. After telling her today that I planned to date and claim her, I was faced with the prospect of having to run. And that meant leaving behind everything I'd earned in the last four years. My club, family, friends, respect, and my girl. Fuck me! Just once, why couldn't life be kind and generous? Was I such a piece of crap that everything I yearned for had to be taken away?

I could not imagine telling Rosie that we were

done. Or leaving without a word. I could not ask Rosie to leave her family or Rage behind and go on the run with me. Sometimes I fuckin' hated life. The burning anger in my gut carried me to my bunk. I swapped nods with my brothers while they sent curious stares. Of course they'd learned about the suit. There were no secrets in Rage. I could see the desire to surround and protect one of their own. But what would they say if they guessed the truth?

I was born and would always be trash. I lusted after a Rage princess who was probably too good for me, but I was too selfish to release her unless forced to. My head cleared slightly once I was in my bunk. The first step was to lose the suit. The second was to speak to Texas, and the third was to keep my past hidden. That meant seeking Dierdre and Clyde and checking what they were up to. I was owed some time off. I'd never taken a holiday or sick day. Drake would let me have a week so that I could investigate. I'd have to find an excuse and make sure it stayed logical.

I turned my attention to the laptop beside me. If I could find a design rally, I could tell Drake I was heading to that. That was the perfect excuse. There'd be no reason to question me. Of course, I'd want to attend and get new ideas. I tapped away and finally found something coming up soon. I bought a ticket and decided to speak to Drake in the morning. It would be too obvious if I went downstairs now, and Drake would attempt to beat the truth out of me.

Rosie was the one who required protection. She

didn't have to understand what she'd got involved with. Once this shit was settled, I'd give her the money to build a clinic. Or better yet, I'd sit down with Apache and Rock, work out a payment system, and get them to build it. Then give Rosie my savings to buy the equipment. That sounded like an achievable plan of action. I needed little to live on, and Rosie already had her own home.

There was no denying I planned to live in it with her, so I could give the guys two-thirds of my earnings and stay solvent. That could only happen when I resolved my past. Dierdre and Clyde could no longer affect me or hang over my head. I was twenty-three and had filled out the promise my body had held. I wasn't a scrawny, weak kid; I was a man with a man's body. If Clyde raised his hand to me this time, I'd put him on his ass. Yeah, I would ensure they understood the message I would bring.

Then Rosie and I could live sweetly.

Chapter Five.

Calamity

I was busy the next day with a build, but I texted Rosie and asked if she wanted dinner. This morning I'd decided to tell Rosie about Mrs Travis and my so-called parents and then explain that I might have to run. No way was I prepared to leave Rosie without her knowing why. Rosie would live her life wondering and, even worse, possibly blaming herself. And Rosie deserved the truth.

The day crawled by. Drake and Ace were both at the garage, keeping a sharp eye on me. Apache and Rock were supervising the construction of the walls around the new compound. The warehouse had been demolished, and the new building was nearly finished. And that fucker was huge. It was four solid walls reinforced with concrete and brick on the outside. Bullet-proof windows were going into every bedroom possible, and the ground level was having windows in the office and some other rooms.

The basement, which would hold church, a panic room, and the old ladies' meeting room, had no windows. This was the final resort should Rage be attacked. No easy entrance and only two staircases. Both would be easily defendable from those hiding downstairs. The clubhouse was nearly finished, and the protective walls were being built. The walls separating the new compound from the garage and forecourt were a priority. Those fuckers were going to be eight feet high.

Ignoring those watching me, I concentrated on the custom paint job. The build only needed a few tweaks, but layering the colours was tricky. It had a neon blue skull on the right with different coloured purple and blue flames streaming from the back. The left side had a reaper whose primary colour was black but with neon accents, and the top of the tank held a cross. It was a stunning design, and the owner hadn't even looked for another once he'd set eyes on it.

It was six when I finally finished up for the night. The garages had shut their bay doors a good half an hour ago. I needed a shower and to ride. I was picking up Rosie's favourites and wished to know how her day had gone. Rosie had intended to call around and inquire about vacancies. She'd been praying that Steiner and his clinic hadn't blacklisted her, but we could only wait. Once I showered, I headed downstairs, and Fish caught me on the way out.

"Okay?" Fish asked, shrewd eyes checking me over.

"Yeah," I responded, not offering any information.

"Where are you heading?"

Ah fuck, I hated lying to a brother.

"Rosie's. Wanna check how the dogs are healing and see if she heard anything." That was some of the truth. Fish's gaze went dark, and I wondered if he'd guessed.

"Hate that shit. Poor canines are so fuckin' loyal, and those cunts deliberately harm them. Hey, I know a man who retrains dogs who've been made to fight. Tell Rosie to text me for Jon's number. Guy has an excellent success rate, and for those that can't be rehabilitated, Jon keeps. Doesn't believe in putting them down as he says it's not their fault."

"Okay, I'll tell Rosie."

"Calamity, good call on catching the dog. From what I hear, it was a horror story out there. Nando's been in touch with Drake and is running the investigation. Ramirez is working on a lead for Santos and has pulled a double homicide. Nothing to do with Rage, but Ramirez is convinced it's dodgy. So keep Nando informed, and I'm happy to let you manage this," Fish said with a nod.

Warmth swelled inside. Fuck if that wasn't trust. Usually, officers took over something, so Drake letting me lead this was fuckin' massive.

"Will do. Better get off. I plan to take a ride later and cruise the area the dogs were dumped in. Got no idea how long ago they were placed there, but a bit of blind luck might happen," I replied, and he nodded.

"Enjoy," Fish muttered and wandered away.

Suddenly, I realised no women were in the clubhouse. The brothers had voted that no more whores were welcome, but the old ladies hadn't returned. I glanced and saw most of the married men were present, and none appeared happy. Blaze, Lex, and Jett were missing. Jett, because he was probably grovelling to Sin, Blaze because he'd be needed on the farm, and Lex because Vivie was pregnant and having a rough time. There was a disgruntled air in the clubhouse, and I hoped the issues would be resolved soon. Shit was too fuckin' quiet.

When I arrived at Rosie's, she'd changed into yoga pants and a tight tee. She looked totally edible, and my mouth pooled with water. Christ, Rosie was the epitome of sex. Rosie smiled at me as I walked towards her carrying takeout. I'd picked up Rosie's favourite Chinese and a bottle of white wine she loved. Briefly, I dropped a kiss on her lips, but as I pulled away, Rosie's eyes shadowed as she peered at me.

"Calam, what's wrong?"

"The past has come back to haunt me, Rosie. But for the next hour, I want to enjoy the meal and relax before telling you everything, and I wish to hear about your day."

"Whatever you need," Rosie said, shutting the door.

A chuckle escaped as Jester tackled my ankles, and

Henrik came barrelling towards me. The enormous dog skidded to a halt and plopped his ass down while looking at me. Quickly, I made a fuss of them both and tickled Empress under her chin. Empress's cute scrunched-up glower caused me to laugh, and I felt better for the first time in twenty-four hours.

"Motherfucker in the house!" Peter shrieked.

"Rude nitwit speaking," Precious retorted, and Peter cawed in retaliation.

Rosie dished up, and we sat at the table in the kitchen, eating and talking about her day. She'd sent out feelers for vacancies and claimed she didn't believe she'd been blacklisted yet.

The lawyer had served Steiner's papers, and now they were waiting for a reply. The fact that the videos existed meant the clinic did not have a leg to stand on. Winnie, Rosie's nurse, was giving a statement, and she'd begged Rosie to find her a spot working alongside her. The wounded dogs had been moved to a different veterinarian. The police ended up being called because Brett had refused to release the canines. Bobby and Dan had marched in with Nando, who had charged Brett and Janine with obstruction. And also threatened to charge them with the destruction of evidence when Brett promised to euthanise them.

Rosie was laughing as we tried to imagine Janine and Brett's fear of being arrested. It served them right. We spent an hour chatting and winding down before I led Rosie to the sofa and took the armchair opposite.

"Hear me out before saying shit. This is going to be difficult. Please try not to interrupt because I won't start again if I stop talking," I asked with fear.

"Promise," Rosie whispered, paling.

"And if you tell me to leave, I will, Rosie. No drama, no arguing, I'll go, baby."

"Calam, if you're about to drop a bombshell, you may have to give me time to assimilate the information. So don't get pissy if I don't reply straight away," Rosie said, and I nodded.

Slowly, I began telling Rosie about my earliest memories of being unloved and going hungry. How I was often abandoned alone and learned crying didn't bring any relief. Images of bullying from when I joined school flashed in my head. Clyde beating the shit out of me because the teacher contacted him and Dierdre about me having no lunch. Carefully, I spoke about the beatings, mental abuse, and how the doctor stopped that bullshit, but Clyde and Dierdre had wheedled me back.

With love, I talked about Mrs Travis and how she terrorised the neighbourhood but took me under her wing. Lovingly, I described how Mrs Travis had loved and looked after me and how I thought she was an angel. That brought tears to Rosie's eyes when the abuse only aroused horror. Rosie listened to how I excelled in school and how Mrs Travis began to fade. The story ended with my attack on Clyde in self-defence and finding Mrs Travis dead.

Rosie was saddened as I explained how I wandered a year, moving from town to town, to stay ahead of any police looking for me. And how unsure I was if Clyde and Deirdre had attempted to set me up on a homicide charge. Rosie was weeping by the time I finished. When I wound down, telling her about the suit who'd appeared on Rage, and I might have to flee, Rosie's expression turned stubborn.

"So, we aren't certain that you're being sought for an alleged murder?" Rosie urged, and I shrugged.

"No, but Clyde and Deirdre would have pointed fingers at me."

"So, let's check. Do you know Mrs Travis's first name and birthday?"

"Yeah, it was Angelique Travis, born 18th of November 1951," I replied as Rosie opened her laptop.

"Where did you live, Calam?" Rosie asked.

"Aberdeen, South Dakota."

Rosie tapped away for several moments and then beckoned me over.

"Is this Mrs Travis?" Rosie sought, and I swallowed hard as I stared at the beloved face of the woman who'd truly been my mother.

"Yeah."

"Okay, let's see what we can discover, Calam."

Minutes ticked past as Rosie searched online, and I watched. Finally, we sat back and gazed at each other in surprise.

"Mrs Travis fell and snapped her neck," I told Rosie.

"But the newspaper report said she had a heart attack."

"I saw Mrs Travis. Yeah, I ain't no doc, but she had

most definitely slipped and broke her neck."

"Calam, the statement says what it does. There's no sign of murder. Maybe we should give the lawyer a call?"

I froze and shook my head.
"Calamity, we need to call and find out what we're dealing with. No lawyer would search for you concerning a homicide. There's no mention of you being wanted anywhere. Hand me the card," Rosie demanded.

Before I knew what I was doing, I'd handed it over, and Rosie dialled his number. Rosie spoke a few sentences into the phone and then disconnected after confirming her address.

"His name is Scott Deverish, and he's on his way. Scott would only tell me it's about your inheritance," Rosie said.

"What money?" I demanded, climbed to my feet, and began pacing back and forth. Had I been running for nothing? Shit.

"Don't know, baby, but he's only twenty minutes away. Scott's coming straight here," Rosie responded calmly.

"Maybe we've made a mistake," I blurted as panic settled in my gut.

Rosie rose and wrapped herself around me.

"Then I'll bang Scott over the head, and you run," she replied, and I snorted.

We sat holding one another until a knock banged on the door. Rosie checked before she let in Scott Deverish. I eyed him warily as he said hello and introduced himself. In return, Rosie spoke for both of us and offered Scott a coffee, which he demurred.

"Let's get down to it, shall we? Mr Tomkins, you're a hard man to find, and your club is protective," Scott stated as he peered at my cut.

Anxiously, I nodded, and Scott smiled.

"Call me Calamity. Billy Tomkins doesn't exist anymore."

"Okay, Calamity. This meeting concerns the final will and testament of Angelique Travis. She willed you everything, and you are an incredibly wealthy young man," Scott announced with a smile.

"Wait, I don't understand," I replied, shaking my head. "I found Mrs Travis that morning. She'd fallen down the stairs and broken her neck."

"Is that what made you run away?" Scott asked.

"Yes. I thought the police would charge me with murder," I answered honestly.

"Not at all. An autopsy was done, and it was discovered Mrs Travis had a massive heart attack. That caused her to fall. Sorry, Calamity, but Mrs Travis was dead before she even began falling; so extreme was the heart attack."

Rosie reached out and held my hand as I assimilated the information. Crap, five years of looking over my shoulder, and Mrs Travis had died a natural death.

"Okay, what do you mean, the estate?" Rosie asked, giving me a few moments.

"Mrs Travis was originally a daughter of Leonard Clements. In fact, she was his only surviving child,

96

and Mr Clements was an incredibly wealthy man. Mr Clements owned the retail chain of Clements Outdoor stores, Clements hotel chain and Clements boiled sweets. Everything, including his wealth, passed to Mrs Travis when he died. She had lost her husband and son in a terrible fire, so she organised trusted people to run the three companies.

"Mrs Travis lived modestly and rarely touched her fortune, so it grew. She also had a canny investment broker who helped enlarge it even further. Mr Tom... sorry, Calamity, you were her sole heir. Mrs Travis left you everything, which includes Clement Hall in Virginia and a mansion in Louisiana. You own sixty per cent of the companies and have over one billion dollars in cash. Calamity, your net worth is well over three billion dollars once the mansions and antiques, alongside the company shares, are taken into consideration."

I stared dumbly at Scott, unable to say a word. I was shocked beyond belief because there was no hint of wealth in Mrs Travis's life. Yes, I knew Mrs Travis was financially stable. But I believed Mrs Travis had a great life insurance policy from her husband.

"Mrs Travis lost a son?" I asked, focusing on the one thing I could handle.

"William Travis was seven when he and his father were in a fire. William passed from smoke inhalation while his parent died trying to rescue him. Such a tragedy and one Mrs Travis never recovered from."

"William, Billy," I announced, putting the two

together.

"Indeed, Mrs Travis took you under her wing, and she left a letter which has never been opened. She told me to tell you it would explain everything. Also, to inform you this, Mrs Travis loved and was very proud of you," Scott added quietly as tears choked me.

Rosie reached out, and I gripped her hand tightly. All the fear and worry fled as I realised I'd allowed Clyde and Dierdre to get into my head. Shit, I'd let those assholes play me once too often.

"Calamity, I need you to sign these documents, and then we could move everything into your name," Scott said carefully.

"Can we have a lawyer check them?" Rosie asked, and Scott nodded.

"Of course, if you could get an appointment as soon as possible, I'd prefer to finish this sooner rather than later. Then you can decide about keeping the companies. Mrs Travis made sure those running them were solid individuals. You can either change or leave them in place. I have copies of accounts and so on that, we'll talk you through. The people in charge get great salaries; Mrs Travis ensured that, so no embezzlement would happen, but you can have your own team check."

"This is too much," I said, squeezing my hands against my temples. Overwhelming wasn't the word.

"Yes, I can appreciate how overwhelmed you must feel. Calamity, take your time and don't make any rush decisions. How you feel today may not be how you'll be tomorrow. One urgent thing I would suggest is you create your own will because without a definite heir, this could cause a legal mess should something happen," Scott urged.

"No need. Rosie inherits everything I own. That will's been around three years," I announced, making Rosie gasp. I turned to her with a smile. "Told you, baby, I always intended to claim you."

After another hour, Scott left, and we sat there staring in shock. A laugh finally escaped me, and I shook my head.

"Fuck, what a day of surprises! Rosie, I need to speak to your dad and claim you. Then I have to inform Rage."

"In the morning?" Rosie asked, eyes wide.

"Yeah, I'll ask Drake to call church," I said, sending Drake a message.

"Would you like to stay?" Rosie offered shyly.

I took her mouth in a searing kiss.

"I'd love to, but not until I've spoken to Texas. Sneaking behind his back is wrong. As soon as we're in the open, I'm going to ravish you, woman," I replied thickly.

Rosie licked her lips and made me groan.

"I'll be waiting."

I was on edge in church the next day. Rosie and the princesses were outside alongside the old ladies. Somehow, they had arrived, knowing something massive was about to happen. I knew Rosie had sought reinforcements in case shit went tits up. Of course, I didn't expect Texas to be over the moon. Rosie was his daughter, but we were in love and serious. I watched as, one by one, brothers filed in while prospects waited outside.

"Can we call them Drake? This concerns them too," I announced and tapped my fingers on my leg.

Drake sent me a surprised look and then whistled for the prospects. Klutz took a stance behind my chair. He knew what was about to happen and was providing silent support.

"Calamity, you called this meeting," Drake mentioned.

I nodded and began telling them about the visit from Scott. A stunned silence fell as I told them exactly what I was worth and which companies I now owned. Happiness shone in Drake's eyes, matched by many brothers as I took them through everything.

"Well shit, congrats, brother!" Drake exclaimed, standing and walking to haul me up and beat my back. One by one, others followed suit before we all sat down.

"Obviously, I wish to share with Rage, but I need to understand the estate. And there is another thing." I twisted to face Texas, who looked surprised and suspicious.

"Brother, I've been in love with Rosie for years. From the moment I saw Rosie, she claimed my heart, and I have protected and watched over her. I want your approval to formally date Rosie," I said, allowing my feelings to leak into my voice. Silence fell like a hammer as brothers squirmed awkwardly and glanced away from me. What the fuck?

"Did I hear you right?" Texas asked.

"Texas, I want your permission to court Rosie," I repeated. "I'm crazy about her and completely in love."

"You think I'd let you claim my daughter?" Texas growled, and I allowed confusion to show.

"The rules are for no hang-ons, candidates, or prospects to date the princesses. But I'm a brother now, one of you." I didn't understand what the problem was.

"We don't say brothers because, by the time you become a brother, you'll realise your brother's daughters are off-limits. Seems that lesson missed you," Texas spat, rising to his feet.

Disturbed, I climbed to mine too.

"Are you saying you'll never give me permission to date Rosie?" I demanded, horrified. This wasn't an outcome I'd considered.

"Never. How dare you think you are good enough to have my daughter? You're nothing but a biker despite this wealth you've come into. Rosie deserves better than a biker, and she'll have that. Withdraw the request now, and we'll move on and forget this and consider it a lapse of judgement," Texas growled.

"Texas, I said I fuckin' love Rosie. This isn't about a lay. I want to build a life with Rosie, watch her dreams come true, help her achieve everything she wants, and stand by her side. This ain't about me coming into wealth. Rosie and I have always known how we feel about one another. We just did nothing out of respect for you and because I wasn't a full brother," I yelled. I couldn't believe this.

"Touch my girl, and I'll see you in hell. My daughter will never court a biker or a member of Rage. Do you fuckin' understand? No piece of shit will walk in and steal my princess."

I reeled back at Texas's harsh words.

"So, I was good enough to bring money in for the club and risk my life several times. But not to date someone I love because she's a princess? So, all I am to Rage is a meal ticket and trash?" I demanded.

Klutz made a strangled noise.

"Yes. Princesses are off-limits. They'll marry nice, decent, smart men, not people like you."

"Trash like me, you mean?" I looked up and sneered.

"Damn right. Money ain't gonna make a difference in the gutter you rose from," Texas roared.

My heart broke at my next action. Blaze and Jett gasped as I shrugged my cut off. I stared at the patch I'd been so proud to win and claim. Broken, I kissed the club's emblem and laid it carefully on the table.

"Then vote. Don't matter what you say. I want and need Rosie, and she feels the same. If you don't want Rosie dating a biker, take my cut, and I'll walk. But none of you shall share my life again," I said and walked out the door.

As I entered the rec room, I saw all the old ladies looking shocked and horrified. Rosie raced across the floor and flung herself into my arms. She was crying.

"We heard everything," she sobbed, wrapping herself around me. Footsteps stomped behind me, and I squeezed Rosie before turning to see the inner circle.

"Take your fuckin' hands off my daughter," Texas growled.

Violence was brewing, and we could all sense it.

"Daddy!" Rosie cried, reaching out to Texas.

"Step away from Calamity. He's a dead man. Calamity broke the code and will pay," Texas thundered.

Penny gasped as she paled and clutched Phoe, who looked appalled.

"I love him!" Rosie shrieked.

"You don't know what love is!" Texas bellowed.

"We've waited four years to be together. And you have the audacity to tell me we don't understand what love is?" Rosie demanded, wiping her tears.

Shit, Rosie's temper was rising. I placed a hand on her shoulder, warning her not to lose it.

"You lust after him. Boy's probably a walking STD," Texas sneered, glowering.

"None of you can name a bitch I've brought to the clubhouse in the last three years," I yelled. "Or say a night I stayed out. Not fuckin' one of ya, and if you do, I'll call liar. I remained loyal to Rosie and haven't touched a woman!"

"You're a liar!" Texas roared and swung.

Hurriedly, I stepped back out of his reach and yanked Rosie behind me.

"Stop," Drake shouted. "We'll vote."

"You vote Calamity out; we are finished," Rosie hissed. "And I mean done. Calam's everything good and loyal about Rage. You determine Calamity is anything but out for loving me and respecting Dad enough to wait until he was a brother and I won't acknowledge or speak to any of you again. You elect for Calamity to leave, then you're a bunch of assholes. Who do you think we're going to date? We've been brought up in an MC life. Expect a doctor or lawyer to cope with that? Jesus Christ, wake the hell up before it's too late!" Rosie yelled.

Texas said nothing but sent me a death stare.

"Back inside and vote," Drake ordered.

I waited outside on tenterhooks, knowing my future was being decided right now.

Drake

"Ain't discussing shit. Candidates and prospects ain't allowed a voice but can remain present. The majority will win. All those in favour of voting Calamity out for disrespecting a brother, hold your hand up."

Gunner, Rock, Texas, Axel, Lex, Lowrider, Apache, Ace, Fish, Slick, Manny, and Ezra, put their hands up.

"Ain't gonna vote against Calamity for falling in love. After what just went down with me and Casey, I'm gonna believe in Calamity," Mac said as Texas glowered at him.

"Mac," Texas growled.

"No, brother, you're wrong and you know it deep down. I stood by Casey when you all turned against her. It was fucking lonely. Ain't doing that to Calamity," Mac insisted. He folded his arms signalling the end of the conversation.

I stared at the younger generation, who steadfastly kept theirs down.

"Those who disagree, raise your hands," I announced.

Blaze, Hunter, Slate, Jett and Mac raised theirs.

"The ayes win. Calamity is out," I said with a hollow feeling in my gut. I hadn't voted because this would fall on my head to kick Calamity from the club as president. Klutz stepped forward as I rose to my feet. The look on Klutz's face was agony as he took his cut off and repeated Calamity's actions. I was stunned as Klutz laid it on the table.

"What the fuck?" Axel boomed.

"I'm in love with Aurora Victoria, and she feels the same. But as a prospect, I stayed away out of respect for the club rules. This bullshit means that as long as I wear a cut or am a Rage member, I can't claim the woman I love. You said no discussion, Drake. You should have had one… because it's too late. Because if the women we cherish mean more to us than our cuts, brothers, family, and loyalty, then we truly worship them.

"Rage wished to build a club with personalities like Calamity. And now you toss us aside because we dared to fall in love with a princess? We break our backs for a few years as candidates and then two more as prospects to prove our allegiance to the club and yourselves. And you call us trash because we cherish a woman you deem us not good enough for. What the fuck are we killing ourselves for? Thought we'd earn respect. Calamity waited four years to claim Rosie, me waiting months for Aurora, and you shit on our feelings.

"Yeah, Texas, we're trash, ain't we? The same as each of you, and like you, us trash would kill to protect the women we love. We would give up everything to be with them. None of ya thought of that when you voted against Calamity. Rage just lost the best of us. You'll never get that kid's like again," Klutz said and strolled out.

I stared as anger rose inside. Unsure of who it was aimed at, I climbed to my feet and walked out, the inner circle behind me and brothers behind them.

Prospects and candidates brought up the rear. Blaze, Jett, Hunter, and Slate all moved to one side apart from us. Making it clear they had not voted in agreement. Sin, Mina, and Ali-kat nodded at their men.

Calamity stood calmly with Rosie tucked into his side. Rosie was paler than him, and I felt a moment of doubt. Behind them, with a hand on each of their shoulders, were Klutz and Aurora Victoria, close by.

"The vote was to declare you no longer a member of Rage," I announced firmly.

Calamity remained tall, but Rosie staggered. Texas went to claim her, and Rosie sent him such a look of venom he paused mid-step.

"You are all dead to me. Rage MC is no part of my life," Rosie spat with pure hatred.

"Baby girl, you gotta see he's trash…" Texas stated.

"Fuck you, Texas. Stay away from my man and me," Rosie hissed.

"Rosie, I'm your dad. Don't call me Texas. You ain't gonna let no guy come between us," Texas expressed with a laugh.

"Watch me. Any of you step foot on my land, and I'll have you arrested. You are dead to me, all of you. And one day, you'll regret throwing Calamity away," Rosie said.

Calamity, Rosie, Klutz, and Aurora left the clubhouse as silence fell.

"I've never been so ashamed of you. Do not come home tonight. You are not wanted," Penny spoke into the silence.

Texas looked shocked.

"Penny, come to the Hall. All of you who wish to leave this bullshit are welcome," Phoe announced, stepping up. Her eyes were narrowed in pure disgust.

"We raise our daughters to be strong and proud. Who do you think they would date? A lily-livered doctor? A bookkeeper? Someone who can't stand up to them or us? Do not come home, Drake, because, as of now, Reading Hall is no longer ours. It belongs to the old ladies, children, and princesses. We do not wish to see or speak to any of you for the foreseeable future," Phoe hissed.

My head shot up at the tone of her voice. She was

beyond angry.

"You need to remove your head from you ass Drake. I know you're resistant to change, we all know that. But you keeping the MC in the dark ages is going to work against you. Wake the fuck up because you lose the club and everything you hold dear!" Phoe continued. On Drake's face was the resistance that Phoe had pointed out. Drake was going to dig his heels in because he didn't want to be wrong. But looking closely at his eyes, you could see he already knew it.

One by one, women began leaving the clubhouse, following their queen bee.

"And Bulldog returns to Rage in the form of Drake Michaelson. What? This crap with the whores is something Bulldog would have done. And the same with Calamity. So much for Rage growing. You're still under Bulldog's bullshit. Fish, until you grow a spine and do what is right, I don't want you near our kids polluting them with this shit," Marsha said, hitting hard and low.

"Marsha!" Fish exclaimed.

"You shame me, all of you," Marsha stated and left.

We stared at each other in confusion and fear.

Blaze, Jett, Hunter, and Slate walked past us without even giving a look. It was obvious where they were going. To my surprise, Gauntlet, Savage, Tye, Carmine, Harley, Wild, and Cowboy followed them. Disagreement showed in every line of their bodies.

"What have we just done?" Axel whispered into the silence.

Chapter Six.

Calamity

I walked out of the club feeling like I'd been hit by a juggernaut. Texas had taken my family away. Everything I'd gained in four years was gone because one man didn't want a dirty biker touching his daughter. Rosie was stone-faced. Dazed, I stood in the forecourt and wondered what the fuckin' hell to do. Klutz was with us, without his cut, and I knew he'd turned it in too. We'd both just lost our family.

"Fuck," I hissed. "We've lost everything, our families, jobs, and home."

"No Calamity. Because as long as I live, you'll have us, and we all feel the same," Phoe spoke from behind. Gathered with her were the old ladies and princesses. Standing next to them were Jett, Blaze, Hunter, and Slate, the prospects and candidates.

"This is going to split Rage," Hunter added, and I

shook my head.

"No, you go back. Hunter, you don't need to do this," Rosie declared as she snuggled into my side. I wrapped an arm around her tightly. Maybe I hadn't lost everything.

"Yeah, we do. What if I fall for Jodie or Serenity? Then I'd be in an identical position to you," Slate said. "Not that I have!" Slate followed up quickly with a sharp look at Phoe.

"Slate, if you took one of my daughters, I would be proud to call you son," Phoe stated, and Slate ducked his head.

"We stand together, brother. You came a little after us, but you're still one of us. I don't give a shit about what they voted in there. They cannot decide who we fall in love with. Rage can't tell me who the hell my family is. And Rosie and Klutz were right. Rage just lost their shining star," Blaze expressed as Ali-kat threw herself into his arms.

"Knew you'd vote the correct way," Ali gasped as Blaze wrapped her in his embrace.

"Fuck, I would never leave a brother standing alone. That's the oath we swore when we joined. The old timers turned their backs on us," Savage commented. It was rare for Savage to speak. Much like Gauntlet, he preferred to be quiet and watch. But when they did, people listened.

"Everyone to Reading Hall," Phoe announced.

"Got to collect the kids," Marsha replied, and several old ladies muttered the same.

"Okay, guys, choose a woman and go with them.

Pack their bags and make sure their idiot husband doesn't interfere. Meet us back at Reading Hall. Security will be put on alert; no Rage is allowed inside bar you lot. Drake made a huge mistake tonight and needs to wake the fuck up. God knows what's going on in their brains. They claim they're moving forward, yet the past influences Rage so much still," Phoe added, shaking her head.

"Hey, we don't want you to do this," I responded, speaking up. I didn't wish to be the reason Rage split.

"Calamity, what I just witnessed was beyond farcical. You have family, and you aren't alone. And as a family, we're going to stand right by yours and Rosie's side. Anybody can see you're both nuts about one another. And what Rage did tonight was wrong. None of them questioned how in love you are. Nope, just jumped the gun. Well, fuck them. Old ladies have suffered a lot of shit. Rage did not care and would get horny when we fought. As you pointed out, Calamity, none cared we were fighting because we were hurt," Artemis said.

I didn't think it was me that stated that, but I'd started the argument that had led to that point.

"It's time those Neanderthals learnt a lesson. We don't want a say in the club, but we fuckin' demand to be respected," Autumn agreed.

"Move, ladies, and I expect everyone at Reading Hall in two hours. Circle the wagons, people," Phoe ordered.

Worried, I swapped glances with Klutz, who nodded.

"Calamity, I won't go anywhere," Klutz vowed as Aurora hung onto his arm. That had been my fear. That Klutz would run.

"Brothers," I announced and stuck a hand out. Klutz grabbed hold and yanked me in close.

"Fuckin' forever," Klutz promised.

"Phoe, Rosie has a shitload of pets. We can't leave them overnight," I suggested to the queen bee, who was very much in her element.

"Then bring them," Phoe said, and I laughed.

I wondered what everyone would make of Peter and Precious.

Rosie

As Calamity and I packed the animals and everything they'd need inside my SUV, I shook at the confrontation with my father. I couldn't believe he thought about Calamity like that. When we first heard raised voices, I'd not paid much attention until Dad began laying Calamity out. Tearing at the deep wounds Calamity held. Fury rose as we listened to Dad's opinion. My heart ached for what my father said to Calamity and how cruel he'd been. Dad, no Texas as I needed to think of him now, had been a total asshole.

Calamity came back from carrying Jester, Terence, and Harold in the car. The last four to go in were Dawn, Fanny, Layla, and Henrik. The rest had already been placed safely inside. Somehow, we crammed a suitcase of clothes in, too. And shit, I realised Calamity had nothing to pack. All his belongings were at Rage. Then I snorted. Calamity was a billionaire now; he could replace everything easily. Once the animals were locked down carefully, I drove out of my lane and towards Reading Hall. Calamity rode behind, protecting me as always.

On arrival, chaos reigned. Kids were racing everywhere, adults rushed back and forth, and security was out in force. Several years ago, Phoe erected wrought-iron gates for Halloween, and she'd left them up, and there was a guard box next to them now. To my surprise, four guards lingered at the gate, checking who was coming in. Phoe had been deadly serious when she'd said Reading Hall was off-limits to Rage. In front of me were Mina and Hunter, and as I waited, I saw Silvie arrive with Savage behind. Fuck, this was really happening.

I'd been shocked when the old ladies had walked after the trouble with the skanks. But when after a week, they hadn't returned to the clubhouse, Drake and the others had finally banned whores. They are making a second strong stand. But this one was more costly. Because I understood, now Calamity had been kicked from Rage, there was no returning for him. Once excommunicated, there could be no return. Calamity and Klutz were literally drifting in the breeze.

But not alone.

I stared as Micah raced down the front steps at

Reading Hall and collided with Calamity and held him tightly. Micah reached out and dragged Klutz into the huddle.

No, they wouldn't be left in the wind to drift aimlessly. They still had family.

We'd make sure they wouldn't ever be lonely. Because that was Calamity's main fear. His deep, dark terror. Apart from Mrs Travis, he'd never had anyone. I would never allow Calamity to be alone again. I swore to fill Calamity's life with colour, love, and family. That was one thing Texas had taught me. Family was what you made. Blood didn't always mean something, but those you collected and chose as family were precious.

Calamity

It had been five days since the blowout at the club, and the old ladies were firmly bunkered down in Reading Hall. Alison and Blaze had returned to the farm because it was getting near their busy season. Hunter and Mina, alongside Jett and Sin, had also gone home. But now, instead of going to the clubhouse to meet up, they came to Reading Hall, or we all met at the Reading Nook. Anyone from Rage trying to get to Reading Hall had been sternly turned away, including Drake.

The old ladies had completely shut their men down. They refused to accept calls and speak to them at work. I felt bad because this situation was causing a strain on many marriages, and with all the damn pregnancies about it, it had to hurt them. Vivie was so ill at seven months pregnant that she was locked up at Reading Hall, and Phoe had hired a nurse.

Lex should be by her side, but Vivie spat, with typical French passion, every time Lex's name was mentioned. When Vivie had spoken to him, she let loose a stream of French that made us all blink. While we couldn't understand it as Vivie spoke so fast, there was no doubting the emotion behind her words nor the fact she was cussing Lex out.

Artemis was now six months pregnant and had discovered it was twins. She hadn't told Ace, which would hurt in the long run. Artemis was silently fuming at having twins again, although we all ribbed her badly. Carly was five months along and, luckily, only with one. I could imagine Rock was screwing at missing out these past few days. Sin was also five months and glowing but was tired and grumpy.

Silvie remained in her wheelchair, and I know Phoe was as worried as I was. Silvie was in such pain. Alison was six months pregnant, with only a day between her and Artemis's due date. Blaze tried to carry Ali-kat everywhere until she took a horsewhip to him, and he backed off. We'd discovered Autumn was twelve weeks gone, and yesterday there'd been an impromptu party when Lindsey announced she was also carrying. Which made Lindsey scowl because she was adopting a little boy and girl who were siblings.

Rosie and I were returning home today. The animals had caused chaos, and Peter had taught the kids a few new swear words. The lawyer had seen me and confirmed all paperwork was legitimate, and we'd handed everything back to Scott four days ago. My bank account had many more zeros than I thought possible when I looked at it the next day.

Rosie and I had sat and spoken, and we had discovered the land to the side and behind her had gone up for sale, and we'd bought it. We had an architect coming tomorrow to speak to us about building a clinic, and we were speaking about what else we could do. Rosie contacted the rehabilitation guy who'd been recommended, Jon, only to discover he was being evicted from the land he rented. On exchanging a glance, Rosie offered Jon space at our place to continue his good work.

Rosie suggested signing the land over to Jon for as long as he worked in recovering abused dogs. Jon was already on his way down to us, as time was a priority, and he needed to access the land. Rosie also planned to open a sanctuary for any abused or abandoned animals. Winnie, the nurse from her old clinic, was coming on board and had handed in her notice. Rosie was giving a higher wage and a far better package than Steiner.

As the lawyer for my companies, Scott was planning to move to Rapid City. He was helping us with all the paperwork needed to get the veterinary clinic, sanctuary, and rescue centre approved. Scott had explained he was my personal lawyer like he'd been for Mrs Travis.

I'd not yet opened her letter, as I could not cope with what was inside.

There was too much emotion and upheaval. Scott had made me sign a document, though. Which gave Rosie my care of life decision-making and naming her to run everything in my absence. Rosie had fought against this, but I explained whatever I had was hers, and she better get used to it. She'd pouted for six hours before agreeing. So, some stuff was settled, and other crap remained the opposite.

The hurt I'd experienced at being kicked from Rage still was as sharp as the day it had happened. And I knew Klutz felt the same. Klutz was coming to work with us. To our surprise, Klutz had registered at college, and with his medical background, he'd been a shoo-in to study as a vet. The talk was he might pass within a year because Klutz already held a lot of knowledge.

Rosie had been filling my ears with equipment, hiring staff for the clinic and rescue centre, and whatever else came to mind. I loved hearing Rosie say what she wanted to do with the money. The companies we'd decided to leave be and let those running them continue to do so. Neither of us was interested in being businesspeople. Scott informed me I'd have to attend each company for one week a quarter, and I'd agreed.

Jett and the others remained supportive, spending time between Reading Hall, Rage, and their families. Whatever was happening at Rage wasn't making anybody happy, but we didn't discuss it. I overheard Hunter discussing how Rage was reeling from Klutz and me handing in our cuts. Nobody had believed it would come to that, and everyone had expected me to give Rosie up. Well, now they knew I'd never abandon Rosie. Rosie was mine. I smiled as the woman of my thoughts appeared, hair swinging in a ponytail and trying to make Henrik get into the SUV.

Chuckling under my breath, I hurried to help.

Rosie

I was surprised to receive a message asking me to attend my old clinic. They had some paperwork they needed to give me concerning my previous employment. I checked with my lawyer before sending a text that I'd go but wouldn't discuss the lawsuit I'd levelled against them. The appointment was for later today after receiving an affirmative reply. That was once I got Henrik's big ass into the SUV. The other animals watched, I felt with amusement, as I bribed the big dog and nudged, and Henrik didn't budge. Calamity strode towards me with a smirk, and Henrik turned his head.

"Henrik, car now!" Calamity ordered, and blow me, Henrik leapt up into the backseat and shoved Layla aside. Irritated, I slammed the door shut and offered my disobedient canine a glare.

"Seriously?"

"What can I say? Rosie, I'm the dog whisperer," Calamity teased as I frowned.

While I sulked, we said goodbye to everyone and promised to come for a cookout on Saturday. Phoe hugged us tightly and told us not to be strangers. Penny whispered in our ears how much she loved us and how proud of us she was before letting go. It upset me that Penny had been hurt during this drama, and she'd seen Texas in a different light. Hell, I never wished that for my wonderful stepmom. As I climbed into the driver's seat, Calamity mumbled something to Penny before kissing her cheek and getting in beside me.

"What did you say?" I asked as I drove down the road.

"Told Penny if she needed us, then to call. Even to help with the kids."

"Has to be hard, especially with Lilah and Nathan. They must be confused."

"Yeah, but we'll make sure Lilah and Nathan know they're loved," Calamity said, glancing out the window.

Calamity's lip curled as I saw what he did. Texas sat on a bike outside the gates. Texas stared as we passed, but none of us acknowledged the other. I felt a stabbing pain in my gut. That was my dad, yet Texas couldn't see past his prejudice. It was fuckin' hurtful that shit had come to this.

"Oh, I had a message. They need me to collect some papers from the clinic to do with my final paycheck. Will you be okay getting the animals soothed and fed?" I asked.

"Rosie, I'd rather attend with you in case that prick is still present," Calamity disagreed.

"Brett won't be. I doubt they'll let Brett anywhere near me," I replied.

Calamity thought it over before giving me a sharp nod.

"Baby, my gut says not to leave you, but I don't want to smother and destroy what we have. If you haven't called me by five fifteen, I'll ride," Calamity offered as a compromise.

I nodded in agreement.

I entered the clinic dead on five and walked to the desk. Chelsea was just collecting her bag and sneered. I returned the expression, and Chelsea blanched. God, I must be frightening.

"Chelsea, I was asked to pick up some paperwork," I announced, tapping my nails on the counter.

"Don't know nothing about that," she muttered, giving me the evil eye.

I sent Chelsea a dirty look in return, and she flinched again. Yup, bitch two, wimpy whore zero.

"Fine, I'll go through to Janine," I said and turned on my heel.

"Biker skank," Chelsea whispered.

I spun, grabbed her by the throat and hauled her half over the counter.

"This biker whore can make you bleed, scream, and beg for death. Don't fuckin' tempt me. Just because you're female doesn't mean I won't make your death bloody and painful. Keep your mouth shut or pay the consequences." Calmly, I stood back, released Chelsea's throat, and smashed her straight in the jaw.

Blood flew from her lip as she squealed.

"That was your one and only warning bitch," I said and walked away.

Angry, I strode to Janine's door and knocked before entering. To my surprise, Janine wasn't there. I frowned and wandered to Dr Steiner and repeated my actions. Again, the office was empty. Anger rising at wasting my time, I moved to back out of the room when a shove sent me sailing forward.

I hit the desk hard, turned around, and saw Brett in front of me. Brett was glowering, and there was madness lurking deep in his eyes. Shit. This was a fuckin' trap.

"What do you want?"

"Drop this suit. You're ruining the clinic and my reputation," Brett snarled.

"Then you should have kept your hands to yourself. No means no asshole," I retorted. The anger remained in my gut, and something told me I would need it. A quick glance at the clock informed me five minutes had passed since I arrived. In ten minutes, Calamity would ride.

"Stop the fucking suit!" Brett roared.

"Why the fuck should I?" I screamed back.

"You wanted me to touch you, said no, but those eyes and lips of yours read yes. Admit you lied and lead me on, and I'll let shit drop," Brett offered, and I stared in disbelief.

"Hawthorne's have multiple videos of you touching me and me telling you to leave me alone. Why the hell should I stop? You touched me without permission, and I warned you repeatedly. Brett, I didn't want you to touch me!" I yelled back.

"Drop the suit, Rosie."

"No."

"Well bitch, if I'm going to be sued for fucking accepting what you put on offer, then maybe I ought to make sure I got my money's worth," Brett drawled. Then he kicked the door shut. Brett was beyond insane with anger. I darted around his uncle's table, putting it between us, and I hit the panic button Dr Steiner kept there. Either Brett didn't know or did not care because he continued closing the distance.

It became a macabre game. Brett feinted right, so I dodged left and then vice versa.

Finally, Brett had enough and pushed the desk, winding me and making me stagger backwards. Brett came around and pinned me against the wall. Hands ripped my blouse open, and Brett grabbed at my breasts. I immediately head-butted him, jumping upwards and smashing his jaw together as I caught him under his chin. Brett's height worked against him. I kicked Brett's shins as he staggered, and I slipped away. Fingers latched into my hair, dragging me back as I struggled and fought. I shoved an elbow into his stomach, forcing Brett to release me momentarily, and moved for the door.

Brett caught me halfway and attacked harder as he

123

nudged me towards the table. My blouse split further, and Brett pushed me over the desk and slammed my head into it. That hurt. I kicked backwards and bucked as he pulled at my pants. A second slam dazed me, and I felt blood flow from my nose. Shit. My trousers ripped with an audible tear, and I noticed Brett's fingers prying between my legs. No way. Not fuckin' happening while I had air in my lungs.

I reared up and smashed my head into his face, and Brett released me with a roar. My hand scrabbled for something, anything, on the table and grasped an item, and I twisted and hit him in the face with it. Brett staggered back as I swung a second time and knocked him clean out. Brett fell to the floor as I wiped my nose and collapsed in a heap next to the desk.

I was sobbing as I raised the hand to my face and stared at what I held. A hysterical giggle escaped as I saw his uncle's bronze award for being nominated as the vet of the year. I dropped it and tried to gather the remains of my blouse together. Brett groaned, and his eyes flickered, and he focused on me and suddenly lunged at me. I swung up and caught Brett on his temple with my weapon, and Brett collapsed backwards as I kicked him.

I sat there watching, waiting for him to move when the office door was booted open, and a guy came in with his gun outstretched. Moving away into a corner, I screamed.

"Fuck! Rosie, it's Dan, Dan Horton," the man cried, and I peered through my fingers.

With a wail, I crawled across the floor as Bobby Lucas entered and dropped close to me. I nearly climbed into his lap as his arms comforted me.

"Call Calamity!" I wept as I burrowed into Bobby's warm body.

"Max, it's Dan. We've got Rosie. An ambo's coming, and somebody phone Calamity," Dan ordered, glancing up at the ceiling.

Fuck, everything had been captured. Brett would be criminally charged this time! As Dan rolled Brett onto his stomach, the camera blinked its red light twice and handcuffed him.

"Rosie, can you talk, honey?" Bobby asked as he held me.

"Brett attacked me. He demanded I withdraw the lawsuit, and when I refused, he said he might as well take what he was being blamed for. Shit, the motherfucker tried to rape me," I answered as reality set in. I began shaking madly in Bobby's arms as I heard someone calling, and Dan replied.
A female paramedic crouched in front of me and began asking me questions as she started checking me over. Her partner worked on Brett.

"We've called a second ambo. We are not putting the victim in with her attacker," Bobby stated to the paramedic working on me.

"Thanks," I replied.

"Rosie!" the roar echoed through the clinic, and the paramedic jumped and looked towards the door, worried.

Calamity ran in and skidded to a halt. Calamity

took one look at me, curled in Bobby's lap as the paramedic worked on me and then at Brett. Before anyone could stop him, Calamity flew across the room, and he kicked Brett in the ribs. He raised his foot again, and Dan swung him around.

"Deal with Rosie!" Dan roared in Calamity's face.

Calamity froze and then dropped to his knees and crawled towards me.

"Baby, are you okay?" Calamity crooned, dropping his threatening tone.

"Hold me," I gasped out as Calamity sat his ass down, and I launched at him.

"I'll always be here for you," Calamity soothed, stroking my head.

Meanwhile, I knew for damn sure he was giving Brett the evil eye over my shoulder. Dan visibly shuddered as two more cops arrived. After several long minutes, I was placed on a trolley and wheeled out. Brett remained unconscious, but no one seemed in a rush to help him. Calamity held my hand as I was moved outside. As we exited, I noticed Janine and Dr Steiner standing in the car lot, alerted by sirens something had happened. They gasped when they saw me, and Calamity sent them a death stare.

A wail escaped Janine as I was loaded up into the first ambulance, and I saw Brett being wheeled out and handcuffed to a trolley. Brett's face was a mess from where I'd head-butted and beaten him, and he remained unconscious. Bobby was talking to them both, and I overheard Bobby say the clinic was off-limits to them as it was a crime scene. Janine demanded to go with Brett and was denied as Bobby informed her he was a suspect and under arrest. As the ambulance's doors shut, I closed my eyes and thought, fuck their asshole practise.

Calamity

I was sitting by Rosie's bed while we waited for her MRI scan to return. Rosie seemed to have a concussion, but Doc Paul had run further tests to ensure she was okay. Apart from a sprained wrist and bruises, Rosie insisted she wanted to go home. And Rosie wasn't playing around, sulky and mulish, I was seeing a side I'd not seen before. Steadily, I raised an eyebrow, and Rosie pouted.

"So, I suck at being a patient," Rosie snarled, and I held my hands up.

Suck was not the word that crossed my mind.

"Calamity!" Rosie growled in warning, and I snorted in amusement. She could have her bitch fit. She was alive and intact. That's all that mattered to me. Booted feet stomped down the hallway, and Rosie stiffened. The door flung open, and Texas, Drake, Apache, Axel, and Axe stormed in.

"What the fuck happened?" Texas demanded, and Rosie pointedly looked away.

"Phone security, they are not welcome here," she stated, and I hesitated.

Texas scowled at me.

"Rosie, wanna tell me why I got cops telling me an ex-colleague of yours attempted to rape you, and you're in the hospital?" Drake sought, holding up a hand to silence Texas.

"Hello, I meant it when I said call security." Rosie's voice was like ice.

She twisted her head and stared at Drake.

"Calamity and I are no longer Rage. You are not welcome here. Now leave before I have you arrested."

Fuck me! Stunned, I froze at her words. Rosie was deadly serious.

"Rosie, speak to us," Texas growled.

A nurse bustled in and gazed around with wide, startled eyes.

"Please call security. These men are bothering me and refuse to go. No one other than Calamity is allowed access," Rosie spoke, still as cold as ice.

Rage exchanged concerned looks.

"Ma'am, Rosie is my daughter. She's clearly suffering from a knock on the head, so can you update me on her condition," Texas urged with ladles of charm.

"Speak to any of them about my medical needs, requirements, or history, and I shall sue. I have disassociated myself from them, and they are no longer my family or in my life. Now, I have asked once for security. If I am forced to ask again, I will file a private lawsuit against the hospital and yourself. These men are not welcome here."

Rosie met Drake's eyes.

"I warned you that should you vote to kick Calamity, you'd lose us both. That was not an idle threat. It was serious. It's not my fault you think because you have dicks you can ruin lives and bulldoze your way through any obstacle. I meant exactly what I said. Calamity chose me over his club and family. How could you expect me to do no less? Now go!"

"Please leave, or I shall have to call security," the nurse stuttered.

One by one, they turned on their heels and left.

"Inform RCPD that I am no longer a member of Rage. What happens to me stays off their radar if it involves the cops," Rosie said, and I nodded.

Fuck, I loved this woman.

Chapter Seven.

Rosie

I was steaming when Texas and Rage left.
Calamity stood in the corner, looking like I was going
to shout, and sorrow rushed through me. This was the
first time he'd seen Rage since they took his cut, and
nobody had acknowledged him. That hurt Calamity,
and I could spy the pain in his eyes. Calamity had
called Rage brothers for four years, and they couldn't
even say hello? Fuck Drake and Texas.

"Calam, shall we go home?"

Calamity looked at me with worry, replacing the
wound.

"Wait for the doc."

"Calam, I'm sorry Rage treated you so badly. The
shame is at Rage's feet, not ours. We did nothing
wrong and everything right. The fact Rage can't see
past their archaic noses isn't our fault. Who the fuck

do they expect the princesses to fall in love with?"

"Don't know, Rosie, but ain't gonna deny that didn't hurt like shit," Calamity said with tears, which he quickly blinked away.

"Calamity, I'm so sorry," I nearly wailed.

"Never going to blame you for how Drake and Texas acted. Thought the bond of brotherhood went deeper. Clearly, I was mistaken. But Klutz and the old ladies remain. Blaze and those that voted to keep me informed they are still my brothers. Drake and Texas can't force them to cut me off, or they'll walk, too."

I gasped at Calamity's words.
He continued, "Never wished to be the dividing force. Just wanted to go with the flow and take things easy. Marry the lady I love, knock out a few kids, grow old together, and have my brothers around. Instead, we'll do all that except Rage. That's Rage's loss, not ours."

"Calamity, I love you."

"As long as I have air in my lungs, you'll be the only woman for me. Rosie Craven, you are my be-all and end-all. Fuck, that's shit!" Calamity exclaimed, and I bristled. What was?

"Planned to take your surname. That ain't happening. We'll need to pick a different name!" I began laughing at the frustration on his beloved face. Calamity was working himself up over giving me a surname. Yeah, I understood why, but it was the surname, and not the fact Calamity wanted to marry me or knock me up, that worried him.

"Seriously, we'll figure shit out!" I spoke through

giggles.

Calamity rolled his eyes and sighed.

"That's why I still use Calamity. Can't stand the thought of becoming Billy Tomkins again. We could take Travis," Calamity mentioned and lit up.

"That would be a fitting memorial for Mrs Travis. Maybe when we have a girl, we can call her Angelique too."

Calamity brightened with an inner glow, and I knew I'd done right.

When we arrived home, we fed the pets and put them to bed before wandering upstairs. Despite the heavy petting we'd done, Calamity had yet to make love to me. Tonight, I needed Calamity and his body to wipe the images of Brett from my mind. That had been too close a call. But I didn't want Calamity to think I was using him, either. Unsure, I hesitated outside the bedroom while Calamity stared in confusion.

"Rosie, are you okay?" he asked, concerned.

"Calamity, I know why you've held back. Being respectful. But I have Brett's images in my head, and I can't live with that. I need you tonight. Properly. Calamity, I want to make love," I announced cautiously. Heat burned in Calamity's eyes, and his hands gripped my arms.

"Are you sure?" he whispered, aware of the near-rape I had suffered.

"Yes. Please fuck me and wipe Brett's touch away," I begged.

"Anything for you," Calamity replied reverently,

and his mouth descended on mine.

As always, electricity flared, and I sank deep into the kiss. I'd not uttered a lie. I needed Calamity's scent all over me, especially tonight. Calamity gently worked the kiss to higher levels as fingers explored each other's bodies. His hands locked under my ass and lifted me, and I wrapped my legs around his trim waist as he carried me into the bedroom. I yanked his top off as he approached the bed and touched the smooth, inked skin under my palms.

I knew Calamity had full sleeves but hadn't known he had a scroll tattoo across his shoulders. The ink was beautifully done, and as Calamity placed me down, I surged upwards, my mouth exploring his chest. Calamity threw his head back in bliss as I licked his throat. Tonight, I intended to leave my mark to warn other women away. Calamity's cock stiffened against my stomach as I left a hickey.

"Like that, is it?" Calamity chuckled and laid me on the bed. His mouth touched my throat in featherlike kisses, making me cry when he sucked hard, leaving his own claiming mark. Excited, I writhed under his ministrations as he paid keen attention to arousing me.

"Rosie, I've not slept with many women, and I have never made love to one. If I do something wrong, say so," Calamity muttered.

I soothed a hand over his hair.

"We'll find our way," I said and rolled Calamity onto his back. Carefully, I crawled onto him, yanked off my top, and undid my bra. Calamity's eyes focused on the two globes in front of him, and he reared up to palm one while making love to the other with his tongue. I gripped his head as he lavished my boob with careful attention. When Calamity took a nipple in his mouth, I moaned.

"Harder Calamity, make me feel the pinch," I gasped.

Calamity obeyed, and I panted as shocks of pain shot through my tender breasts. Repeating the actions on my other breast left me putty in Calamity's hands. Wetness had pooled between my legs, and I was unashamedly rubbing myself against his hard cock. I traced the contours of his back, loving how the muscles moved under my featherlight touches. Calamity was highly sensitive.

"Let me," I whispered and pushed Calamity down on the bed. I pulled his boots and socks off before undoing his jeans and sliding them and his boxers down his legs. Calamity looked a little shy as my gaze focused on his dick. It was long and thick, and I groaned. It was perfect. I sank down and placed it in my mouth, and Calamity yelled. Unhurriedly, I took him as deep as possible, my hand moving with my bobbing head. Calamity froze as I deep-throated him, and I released him with a pop and stared up at his worried face.

"What is it?"

"I've never had head before. Do I release in your mouth or tell you to stop?" Calamity whispered.

A happy smile crossed my face. I was giving Calamity his first-ever blow job.

"Cum in my mouth. Just relax, Calam," I said, and Calamity's eyes widened.

I spread the wetness and took him again. I kept spreading the wetness around as I sucked him hard and as deep as I could without gagging. Small moans escaped Calamity as I gave him everything I had to offer. His cock twitched a prelude to ejaculating, and I shoved my finger into his soaking wet anus.

Calamity yelled. His hips lifted off the bed, and he almost choked me as I sucked him with my mouth. I pressed on his prostate, and Calamity came. Happily, I sucked him dry and kept teasing him, and he continued coming. Jesus, my man was amazing. Finally, I withdrew my finger and released his cock and straddled him.

"What do you want, baby girl?" Calamity asked, wide-eyed. His eyes were on my bare pussy.

"Your mouth," I demanded.

Calamity didn't hesitate in sliding down and cupping my ass to pull me to his mouth. His fingers and tongue worked me harder than any guy ever had. And I'd had three lovers before Calamity. There'd been none since I met him. I was holding onto the bedframe as mews escaped my mouth when Calamity's finger repeated my actions. Shit, it was so hot. No man had touched my ass, and here was Calamity working me like a pro. The pressure built, and I cried out.

"Calamity, I'm going to cum!" It was only fair to warn him.

Suddenly, Calamity jolted me backwards and

slammed his cock into me. I screamed as his thickness stretched me while his tip hit my cervix. Letting go of all constraints, Calamity gripped and fucked me senseless. I was all feeling and nothing else, and I erupted, tightening my walls around his dick as I felt him spill at exactly the same time. Calamity ground hard into me, and I knew I'd be feeling him still tomorrow.

I collapsed against his chest, and he thrust once more.

"Oh God, I think we might need a break. That was out of this world."

"Baby, I got four years pent up. Who needs recovery time?" Calamity said as his cock stiffened inside me.

"Who needs sleep?" I asked as Calamity began moving lazily.

Calamity

I was smiling as Rosie drove home from Bernard's. After making love all day and washing away any lingering memories of Brett, we'd gone for food. We'd seen Jett and Sin there, and they'd joined us for dinner. Jett was still obviously grovelling to Sin, although his standing by my side had done much reparation in Sin's eyes. Sin made no bones of how she had felt while staying at Reading Hall. We also saw Hawthorne, who offered a head tilt.

James Washington and his wife Kate were present,

enjoying an intimate dinner, and they'd stopped and spoken to us when they left. Washington hovered over his woman protectively. They were open and friendly, and I caught a wink from Washington, meaning that everything was fine as far as we were concerned. Washington wasn't taking sides.

Rosie was full of good food, wine, and happiness on leaving. She was glowing as she babbled about our plans and that she loved what the architect had drawn up. We were searching for a trustworthy firm. Usually, we would have hired BlackRock Construction, Apache and Rock's company. But obviously, they were out. We'd also met the dog recovery expert, and I'd been impressed. Jon knew what he was talking about and was highly dedicated to the animals he rescued and retrained. The guy had a high achievement rate, so we offered Jon the land.

Rosie had animatedly discussed Jon's building needs and what the dogs required, and they'd hashed out a plan with the architect. There would be a large building containing kennels, two offices, and an indoor and outdoor training area. Jon took up a third of the area that Rosie bought, but nobody cared. The rest of the land was being held for the sanctuary Rosie desperately wanted to open. As we climbed in the car, I wondered what my role in this would be. All I knew was how to design custom bikes. There wasn't much call for my skills in Rosie's world.

However, I was bankrolling everything, knowing Mrs Travis would have definitely approved of what was planned. Mrs Travis had been a kind soul and would have loved the money being used for the animals. But that left me feeling empty. I didn't know what I planned to do. As we turned onto the road that led to home, headlights flared, and a truck hit us sideways.

Metal screamed, and there was a sound of smashing glass. Rosie's SUV rocked, and then there was a second impact, and we rolled. The vehicle landed on its tyres, rocking, and I sat there, stunned. Glass and twisted metal surrounded us, and I blinked in shock. Rosie moaned, and I saw two trucks pull up in front. Shit, this was an attack.

"Rosie!" I called as I tried to unlock the seatbelt. Rosie made a noise again as I got the belt undone and wrestled hers.

"Calamity?" Rosie asked, raising a hand to her head. Worried, I noticed a cut on her forehead and winced, knowing she was hurt.

"You need to run. Somebody's trying to take us," I said, kicking at the door. It took four blows before it opened, and as I staggered out, I saw men heading towards me.

Angrily, I grabbed the gun from my shoulder holster and aimed and shot. The approaching guys scattered as Rosie climbed out. She seemed more alert than I was.

"Go, baby," I urged and fired again.

Rosie hesitated, and I saw the fear in her eyes. "Run!" I bellowed.

Rosie finally obeyed and staggered off into the treelines. Relieved, I watched Rosie disappear and began firing. I prayed I hit those assholes on each shot, as I didn't have many bullets.

"Find the girl," a voice called.

"Put the gun down!" somebody yelled, and I fired in that direction.

A shadow moved, and I hit him dead to rights. The target dropped with a cry, and someone else stepped into the moonlight. The next bullet took him out, and then my gun was empty. I readied myself for a fist fight, but that didn't happen.

As I blinked the blood out of my eyes from a wound I didn't even know I had, a bullet took me in the shoulder, and I spun around, hitting the ground.

"Little fucker," a voice growled, and darkness crept over me.

My final image was a face I never wished to see again.

Clyde.

Rosie

I was sobbing as I left Calamity behind. Gunshots echoed, and I knew Calamity was fighting to save me. The shouts of those looking to find me shrieked in my ears, and I plunged heedlessly into the trees. I kept running despite feeling weak and lightheaded and spotted a huge bush. Silently, I scrambled inside and pulled out my phone. Quickly, I texted Nando about what happened and turned the screen dark. The light could lead them to me.

Footsteps pounded nearby, and I curled into a smaller ball. Please don't let them find me, I begged silently. They wanted us both, and my being free was keeping Calamity alive.

"Come out, and we won't hurt you much," a voice chuckled.

Fuck that.

"Girl, get out here. You don't, we'll make it worse for the boy," the asshole snarled.

I froze.

Just as I moved, a yell cut through the darkness.

"Cops! Run, or I'll leave you behind!"

"Understand this. All Billy's gonna suffer is on your head, bitch," the guy sneered and jogged away.

Peering through the bushes, I saw moonlight glance off him, and I spotted a patch as he turned. I gasped in horror and curled up into a tighter ball. Red and blue lights appeared in the distance, and I knew help was coming.

Crying, I yanked out my phone and texted the two men who wouldn't let me down.

"Rosie!" a guy shouted, and I peeked up. I hadn't moved from my hiding place and was shivering with cold and shock.

"Rosie!" a second shouted, and I recognised Nando.

"Nando!" I screamed and crawled out.

"Rosie, keep yelling!"

"Here, Nando, here!" I shrieked.

Frantically, I started to scrabble free. Branches scratched me more than they did when I entered the bush. A flashlight hit as the bush shook with my movement.

"Fuck, what the hell happened!" Nando exclaimed as he hurried over. "Justin, I got her. Rosie's here, and she's hurt." Nando gently reached out and picked me up.

"Saw the car, Rosie. Who hit you?" Nando asked.

I noticed more blue and red lights on the street and at least four cop cars and an ambulance. The bright lights made me flinch, and I spied cops hovering over two bodies in the road. That meant Calamity hit some of them.

"Calamity?"

"They took him, Rosie. Do you know who it was?" Nando sought sympathy on his face.

"No, and Calamity's not protected by Rage anymore. Nando, I think that was the point. Someone's been watching, and while Calamity wore the patch, he was untouchable. Now he's alone," I said with a sob.

Bikes roared, and the people I'd texted skidded to a halt and jogged over. Nando was still holding me when Klutz snatched me in his arms. Micah hit my back as I buried my head into Klutz's throat as tears broke, and I sobbed.

"We'll find Calamity," Klutz promised, and I nodded.
Calamity had to be alive. I couldn't imagine life without him. We had our entire future together. Klutz would find and bring my man home.

More motorbikes roared, and as Micah placed me

on a gurney, I was surprised to see Rage appear. Drake and Texas climbed off their bikes and hurried towards me.

"How is Rosie?" Texas bit out.

"What the fuck happened?" Drake demanded.

Angrily, I held a hand up.

"You don't have permission to tell Rage anything concerning Calamity or me. Nothing, Nando. Rage threw Calamity away and deserves no information."

"Christ. We'll get Calamity back," Drake responded, running fingers through his hair.

"Rage doesn't need to do anything. My family will find Calamity," I replied without looking at Texas. But I saw his body jolt and felt anguish waft off him. Good, maybe Texas finally realised what he'd thrown away.

"Rosie, we are your family," Drake argued.

"No, you were. When Rage voted against our love and future, you became family no longer. Somebody out there has my man, and Calamity's not yours to search for. Rage threw Calamity out, so don't turn up here pretending to care," I retorted.

"Detective, we need to get Miss Craven to the hospital," a paramedic said.

"Klutz, please come with me," I begged.

He nodded and jogged to his bike.

"Klutz talk to us," Drake thundered. Micah and Klutz ignored Drake as I was lifted into the ambulance.

The doors shut on Drake and Texas's sad and confused faces before I was sped away to the emergency room. Only a single pair of pipes roared behind the ambulance.

Two hours later, Klutz was pacing as he listened to my story. Micah was outside on the phone and hopefully he was calling in allies and friends of Calamity. Nando had taken a statement, and an alert had gone out on Calamity's kidnapping. Ramirez had arrived with condolences and informed me he had contacted allies to help. To Ramirez, it didn't matter that Calamity wasn't Rage anymore. They were friends. I had instructed both detectives that Rage was not to be involved as they'd cut us both loose. Both guys looked like they disagreed but nodded.

Nando had just left when Jett entered. He and Klutz swapped a glance and a nod, and Klutz turned.

"What didn't you tell Nando?" Klutz demanded.

"I spied a patch. They were from a club called Lawless Rogues. They hail from the north-east of the state," I answered.

Jett tilted his head and typed on his phone.

"Jett, that better not have been Drake," I said as I heaved myself upright. I had two bust ribs, various cuts and bruises, and a slight concussion. I had made my sprained wrist much worse, and I'd a deep slash across my forehead. To everybody's disapproval, I'd forced the nurses to stitch, glue, and wrap me up. Calamity needed me, and I could shoot as well as anyone. I was going after Calamity, come hell or high water.

Jett's phone beeped, and he sent a reply.

"Everyone's meeting at Reading Hall. Get Rosie discharged and meet there. An hour, Klutz. And no, Rosie, I wouldn't disrespect you like that." Jett said.

I nodded as I swung my legs over the bed. My clothes had been cut off, but Jett had brought some black jeans and a dark sweater. He'd also thoughtfully provided underwear. Klutz helped me dress as I winced in pain. Thankfully, they didn't talk me out of going after Calamity. They treated me with respect. Not like Texas would have. No, Texas would have shouted, bellowed, and bullied me to remain behind and allow the men to wave their cocks about.

When we arrived at Reading Hall, after stopping to collect my sniper rifle, I was surprised to see bikes I recognised. Blaze, Slate, Jett, Hunter, Savage, Gauntlet, Harley, Wild, and Cowboy were waiting inside, and not one wore a cut.

"What have you done?" I gasped in horror.

"What's right? Calamity is our brother. We are not gonna let those assholes have him. And as it's against another MC, we can't wear patches. That would be Rage declaring war against the Lawless Rogues. But as individuals, we can go in," Hunter explained.

A quiet sob left my mouth as Hunter hugged me tightly.

"We're going to bring Calamity home," Hunter promised, and I nodded.

I looked up and blinked as I saw Akemi, Angel, Simone and Butch, Autumn, Lindsey, Artemis, Casey, and Phoe present.

"What's going on? You three are pregnant and are certainly not going!" I yelled.

Artemis stared smugly.

"Oh, we are, but we're gonna be hanging back, picking off strays who venture out and covering their backs," Artemis stated.

"Artemis, no!"

"Rosie, yes. Don't bother arguing. We'll take your boy back," Autumn replied.

"Fuck you, woman, I'm going in with the boys." Casey grinned and signalled to the four silent guys behind her. I recognised Casey's dad, Jacob, and Uncle Gilbert, alongside two of Jacob's men. Out of a doorway stepped James, Washington, and Adam, and with them came Dylan Hawthorne, with Davies, Max, and London.

"We have intel, so let's discover what Nigel and Leila have," Phoe said, and we followed her to the large dining room.

We all crowded in, and Leila rose to her feet as we took seats.

Micah and Klutz sat beside me making a statement.

"This information has been gathered from the moment you informed Klutz about Lawless Rogues. They're a one percenter club established over a hundred years ago. There's nothing they ain't into, protection, arms, drugs, and women, to name a few. The club is as dirty as it comes. We didn't understand why they'd go after Calamity until we discovered this."

Leila turned a laptop, and I frowned at the man's

face.

"His name is Clyde Tomkins, and he is Calamity's father. I've dug as deep as I can in the time allocated. Long story short, when he was young, Clyde was an abusive asshole towards Calamity. An old lady took him in and raised Calamity for ten years. Mrs Travis died from a heart attack, and Calamity ended up in Rage.

"Clyde tried to set it up as if Calamity had murdered her, but the autopsy showed it was a massive heart attack, and the attempt failed. What the parents found about Mrs Travis's worth, they began searching for Calamity. The search stopped two years ago, and we suspect they found Calamity then. But they couldn't touch him because he was protected by Rage and their allies.

"Lawless Rogues run to around sixty men, all based in one clubhouse. Rage and friends outnumbered them, and they didn't want the risk of war. They must have kept eyes on Calamity because ten of them rode out as soon as he was spied without his cut. Calamity is at their compound in Aberdeen," Nigel said, turning his laptop to show a satellite image.

There was an ugly squat building and some sheds. Trees surrounded them, and they had a wire fence. There was a single road in, but the building was disadvantaged. It could be attacked easily from the trees, despite them having cleared a large patch of ground. Far back was a larger brick hut, and Nigel pointed at it.

"That was built as their wet room. Calamity will be there."

"This is the plan," Jacob said, rising to his feet.

In detail, Jacob quickly took us through a simple attack plan. We all nodded as our roles were clarified and then repeated, so we knew exactly what we were doing. Anxiously, I glanced at the clock. Lawless Rogues had held Calamity for five hours now, and we were well into the early hours of the morning.

"Everyone needs to bed down and get some sleep. We'll be leaving at ten. That means we will arrive at around five. We're taking SUVs provided by my team and Hawthorne's, as they are bulletproof. No bikes. The attack is set for seven. That allows us two hours to get situated. Nobody deviates from the plan," Jacob warned with a sharp glance at Casey and Artemis, who assumed an innocent air.

"Rosie, I understand you want to leave now, but attacking in broad daylight is suicide. We need the cover of darkness, and they're after Mrs Travis's money. They'll not kill Calamity off straight away. Clyde will demand him to sign over the businesses, and Calamity won't. He'll know someone is coming for him. Calamity just doesn't realise who," James Washington said.

"I know James, but every hour they have him, they're hurting him," I whispered.

"And they'll pay," James promised.

"Make them bleed," I swore, and James nodded in approval.

Drake

I walked into the clubhouse with the brothers at my back. We'd been riding, trying to discover a lead to Calamity and what had happened, but mouths were tightly shut. I noticed the quietness of the rec room without the women and children present. This rift was killing the married men. They just wanted their women and families. My eyes fell on something on the bar, and I strode over and paled. In front of me was a pile of neatly folded cuts with a note on top. My fuckin' hand shook as I reached down and picked it up.

"Drake. This is not notice of our resignation but an acknowledgement we have a family member in trouble that we can't defend or rescue wearing our cuts. To wear them while bringing Calamity back would be a declaration of war. We don't have the authority for that. The cuts here represent our love of Rage, dedication and respect for the rules, and you as president.

But we swore an oath to Calamity, once when he became a prospect and twice when he turned into our brother. We vowed never to leave a brother behind, and while Calamity is no longer Rage's brother, he is ours. Should we fail, you can distance yourself from whatever disaster fell on us. All we ask is you look after our families.

Should we succeed and bring our brother home safely, we hope you understand why we took our cuts off temporarily. Our actions should not bring war to Rage. But we'll keep our promise to Calamity. We will take whatever punishment the inner circle deems necessary to readdress our disobedience.

Signed: Jett, Hunter, Slate, Blaze, Savage, Gauntlet, Harley, Wild, and Cowboy."

I read the letter out loud and heard exasperated noises around me. I raised my head and caught Ace's glance.

"Call them one by one," I demanded.

Ace and Apache both whipped their mobiles out and began dialling. Minutes ticked past before Ace sunk his head in defeat.

"Those fuckers have all turned their phones off," Ace growled.

I'd already suspected as much.

"They found out who has Calamity. Somehow, they did. Now we need to find our missing brothers," I stated.

"Should we interfere?" Gunner asked quietly.

"Wanna tell Mina, Ali-kat, and Sin why they are suddenly widows?" I yelled and threw an ashtray at the wall.

Fuck this split between us.

Texas and I needed to chat and get his head fuckin' straight.

Chapter Eight.

Calamity

Slowly, I took stock of my injuries. Clyde and his fuckin' MC had beaten the ever-loving shit out of me, and I was in poor condition. All ten fingers were broken, my palms were fucked, and they'd nailed train spikes through my hands to hang me from a beam. Even if I escaped and survived, I'd never work the fine detail on a bike again. If my career hadn't been over, it fuckin' was now. Moving downwards, I knew half my ribs were broken, and I had a pierced lung. How did I know that? Because those fuckers cut me open and put a drain in. Oh no, they weren't about to let me choke on my blood.

My spleen and kidneys were fucked, considering how bruised I felt there. My hips had been burned with brands, and I was a mass of stinking, foul-smelling flesh. One leg was dislocated where they'd hung on it until the hip popped. And both knees had been smashed, and my feet caned. The bullet wound in my shoulder screamed with the salt they'd rubbed into it. Clyde had whipped my back, trying to tear the Rage patch from my skin. If only Clyde knew he was doing Rage's job for them.

So why the fuck was I conscious with these injuries and others I wasn't aware of? Because that bunch of cunts kept shooting me up with adrenaline and keeping me awake. Clyde wanted me to suffer, and I was doing exactly that. I'd lost track of how long I'd been there, but I knew the night had passed. If someone was coming, it was too late now. I was dying. My body had undergone too much, and Clyde still hadn't got what he needed.

And he never would because the stupid fucker had broken my fingers. It was impossible for me to sign over the wealth I'd inherited, and that was what Clyde claimed this was all about. I called bullshit. This was about me escaping Clyde and his enjoyment of beating the shit out of me. Clyde had his men out looking for Rosie, rightly guessing she was the only thing that could break me. And I was pissing Clyde off. I wanted this to end now, on my terms. No more torture.

During the entire time he'd had me, I'd not spoken. No matter how much Clyde and his MC taunted me, I'd kept my lips shut. Apart from the screams of pain. But I'd not uttered a word, which was messing with Clyde's head. When he'd become part of an MC, I didn't know. I also did not see an officer patch, but he obviously held some sway. My eyes closed as I ignored whatever they were planning to do next. Fuck, my face was so battered Rosie would never recognise me again.

"You don't understand. Rage MC and their allies have put feelers out. They're looking for him. You told me that Billy's cut had been striped!" a guy shouted at Clyde, and I opened my eyes.

I didn't have my cut, so there was no way Rage was coming.

"Asshole was kicked from Rage for fucking a princess. Billy isn't Rage," Clyde yelled back.

"If that fucker's not Rage, then why wasn't the patch sliced from his skin?" the other man yelled.

"Pres, he's nothing. Rage might be searching for Billy to grab the money, too. They aren't gonna track Billy to us," Clyde argued.

"Clyde, I give you leeway with this club. You earned us a lot of dough over the years, so you better pray you're right. Because Rage one on one, we could win, even if they bring Hellfire into it. But the other clubs, Juno Group, Hawthorne's, and the rest of the maniacs Rage associate with, we can't fuckin' win."

I allowed a laugh to spill out of me. It made them both jump.

"Rage is coming," I growled through torn vocal cords. "Clyde fucked up, and you're all going to die!"

Worry blossomed in the man's eyes before Clyde started screaming and punching me. Something hard hit my head, and it was lights out.

Rosie

I'd fallen asleep the moment my head hit a pillow, which I now felt was undeserving. Who knew what the fuck Calamity had suffered while I slept safe and sound like a baby? Casey noticed me fretting as we headed towards Lawless Rogue.

"If you fell asleep during the assault, we'd all kick your ass, Rosie. Ensuring you rested to ensure you're in the best working shape possible isn't something to be guilty of. But getting one of us shot because you're injured and tired is," Casey said firmly.

Jacob nodded by her side.

"Any soldier will snatch even ten minutes' rest when possible because he knows ten minutes might save a brother. If we came during the day, we'd all be tired and not at our best. Which means, Rosie, that we may have saved Calamity but possibly lost several of us in his place. Who would you choose to give up their life for Calamity?" Jacob asked kindly but harshly.

I blanched.

"Nobody," I whispered. *Me,* I wanted to shout.

"Then making sure you're rested while you are already injured is not spitting in Calamity's face. It shows you care enough to ensure you're at your best when we retrieve him. And I promise, Rosie, we're bringing your man home. We even have a chopper on standby should Calamity need it," Jacob reassured me.

I nodded quietly as the countryside flashed past as we drove to the rendezvous point we'd picked.

Once there, the teams separated. Autumn and I took one sniper position, Artemis and Lindsey a second, covering both exits. Phoe, Micah and Jason had taken the third wall while Jaime (James's nephew) and one of Jacob's guys held the fourth side. They covered the large windows at the side of the compound that Lawless Rogues might use to escape. Jacob split James, Adam, Dylan, and Max into one team. Akemi, Angel, Butch, and Simone the next.

Casey went with three of Jacob's guys while the second unit of Jacob's headed towards their infiltration point. Blaze, Hunter, and Savage moved to their spot of attack while Klutz, Jett, Wild, and Cowboy, alongside Harley, went to theirs.

Jacob was staying behind, monitoring everything. It had been made plain that we did as Jacob commanded and didn't disobey his orders.

We could see eight to ten men moving about the yard. Clearly, they were guards and were expecting some sort of attack. The smaller building held four more men outside, and I guessed there were more in both buildings. Impatiently, I waited for the teams to get into place. We were surrounding the compound and intended for no one to escape. All of us wore dark mismatched clothing and face paint.

It was a common mistake to wear all black because that stood out. Instead, wearing black and grey or dull colours allowed you to blend in with the shadows rather than producing a black man-shaped object.

After forty minutes, the final team reported that they were in place.

"Teams Echo, Foxtrot, Gamma, and Hotel prepare to infiltrate. Once within one hundred yards of clearance, hold fast," Jacob said.

Somewhere out there, our people moved to come close to the cleared ground. I readied my sniper rifle just as Jacob spoke again.

"Sniper teams, Alpha and Bravo, Charlie, concentrate on the gathering at the front of the building. Sniper team Delta take out the four in front of the smaller building," Jacob commanded. No sooner had the words left Jacob's lips than my finger squeezed, and the man I'd been targeting was downed with a headshot. I moved to the second and fired, achieving a chest wound. I shot a third time and hit him in the head.

So far, not a single sound had been noticed. Using the night vision sight, I scanned the area to see if any were moving or if there was an unexpected target. Autumn tapped my nozzle, and I nodded. She, too, was scanning for further targets. As we'd used silencers, no one knew twelve men were down and dead. I noticed shadows move as the infiltration teams came out of their cover. Autumn and I took over covering Echo. James spun, his gun raised, as a man came out of nowhere. James's revolver fired a mere moment before mine, and the asshole dropped with two bullets. Autumn shot another man heading for Adam.

Foxtrot reached the front doors, and I watched them prepare something. Hotel informed Jacob they were in place, as Gamma did the same. Moments later, bright flashes lit the sky as all three teams threw flash bangs into the buildings. There were staggered gunshots as I waited on hotplates for any news of Calamity. Echo unit crept into the clubhouse, and further bullets were exchanged. Five minutes later, the Foxtrot team came outside and waved an all-clear.

"All dead inside," the leader of Foxtrot confirmed. "Hotel performing another sweep, and Echo will accompany them. We're going to head to the second target location."

"Confirmed," Jacob replied.

My rifle kept sweeping the area, looking for any threats, when Autumn's rifle fired beside me. She'd been covering the doors, and someone had been creeping out of them. I high-fived her and continued protecting Foxtrot's back. There had been no chatter from Gamma since they entered the smaller building, and I felt worry build up. Gamma had been composed of Klutz, Jett, Cowboy, Wild, and Harley.

"Gamma clear, we need the chopper now," Klutz's voice broke the silence, and a sob escaped my throat.

I was up and moving before Autumn could stop me, and I heard Jacob ordering cover for me as I dashed out of the trees and headed to the building. I burst inside, and a scream left my mouth as I saw Calamity hanging from a beam. Under him, supporting his weight with tears streaming down his face, was Jett.

"Calamity's alive!" Wild cried, catching me as my knees went.

"Alive?" I gasped.

Calamity was no longer recognisable as himself. He was a mess of blood and bruises and broken bones. My heart nearly stuttered to a stop.

"Calamity is breathing, but we need to get him to the hospital. Stay strong, Rosie," Harley expressed as the teams lowered the beams.

I gazed around and noticed five guys knelt on the floor. Two men beside them displayed bullet holes in their heads. Over them stood three of Jacob's men.

Calamity didn't moan as they pulled the spikes out of his hands and wrapped them carefully.

"The chopper is on its way. ETA ten minutes at the rendezvous point we chose for it," Jacob's voice came over the mic.

"No, sir. Need it here; the package won't make it if we travel with him through the treeline. Advise bringing straight to compound," Foxtrot leader responded in reply.

"Who are they?" I spat.

"That's Calamity's father and four of the officers. One's the president," Wild answered with a sneer.

"Just put a bullet in us," a guy suggested, and when I looked, I saw his patch said Clyde.

"Take them," I added as Blaze appeared behind me. Blaze cocked an eyebrow. "Let's see how these motherfuckers hold up the torture they performed on Calamity. Take them, Blaze, and no one touches them until I'm present."

Blaze nodded, and Jacob's agreement came over the mic.

"Just put a bullet in us!" the president cried, repeating Clyde's words.

"Not a fuckin' chance. Everything you did to Calamity, we're gonna repay tenfold. And you better hope Calamity makes it because these guys have experience making you last weeks while we dish the pain," I hissed, leaning forward. I slapped Clyde straight across his face. He wasn't looking so smug now. He'd paled.

"How many men did you have here?" Micah asked.

When no one answered, he kicked the president in the head and shot him in the hip.

"Forty-five," he moaned as he rolled on the ground.

"And you believed that would be enough to stop us from coming after Calamity? Fuckin' idiots," Hunter growled.

A truck pulled up outside, and the survivors were hogtied and driven away. Moments later, a helicopter landed, and Klutz, who'd been working on stabilising Calamity, hurried out to it. A stretcher was removed, and Calamity gently rolled onto it. I rushed out with Klutz, who took one look at my face and shoved me on board.

"Stay small, Rosie," he ordered, and I curled into a corner. One of the Delta Force guys climbed in as he and Klutz still worked on Calamity. The chopper took off, heading toward the hospital.

Out of the corner of my eye I saw Phoe offering

comfort to Micah, who stood alone in the midst of a crowd. The agony on Micah's face said everything.

I dialled Doc Paul and Doc Gibbons and demanded they get there. While I understood Calamity needed life-saving surgery, I wanted our doctors on board. Both doctors said they'd be there as soon as possible. That was comforting as we flew towards the nearest emergency room.

Calamity remained unconscious, and I didn't know if he'd live.

Drake

"We got word. A convoy was seen leaving Reading Hall three hours ago," Fish reported, hurrying in.

"Lawless Rogues took Calamity. They intended to grab Rosie and torture her to make Calamity sign over his wealth. Rosie escaped thanks to Calamity giving himself up to save her," Max stated, striding in.

"Lawless Rogues? From Aberdeen? What fuckin' problem did they have with Rage?" I spat. I'd heard of them, but they stayed well away from Rapid City and the surrounding areas.

"Not Rage. They wanted three billion dollars, and we handed it to them when we kicked the kid," Apache surmised.

"Fuck!" I roared.

Guilt flared across Texas's face and then was

ruthlessly shoved aside.

"We ride now. Whoever has gone after Calamity has a three-hour head start on us. We need to catch them up," I ordered.

"Why?" a sweet voice demanded, and we turned to find Penny watching.

Texas moved towards her swiftly, and she held a hand up, disgust on her face. Texas faltered and stopped.

"Penny?" I asked.

"Why does Rage have to ride? Calamity is not one of you. You owe him nothing," Penny said. She was emotionless, and I didn't like it. Penny was never cold and unfeeling.

"Because Calamity is one of us," I replied.

Penny shook her head.

"Calamity's not. He's one of mine, but not yours. You threw Calamity away. That sweet boy who dared fall in love with our daughter," Penny spat at Texas.

We all flinched at the hate and venom in Penny's voice.

"Princesses are off limits," Texas said inanely, and anger flared in Penny's eyes.

"Why? Who the hell do you expect them to date?"

"Anyone but a fuckin' biker? They deserve better than this life. Shit, they need the white picket fence, the two-point-five kids, and a husband who goes to work at eight and comes home at five," Texas roared.

"What a boring life. So, by your thinking, Phoe, Lindsey, Autumn, Carly, and I are all trash. None of us are worth what the princesses deserve. That explains so much. Why you were willing to turn a blind eye to the skanks taunting us. Why you allowed them to come around and brag they'd fucked you. You all ignored our pain but sure as hell got off on it when we fought with one. Shit, we're no higher than the whores, are we? Princesses deserve the world but not your old ladies. We're just good pussy who can give you children," Penny hissed, and horror rose and swamped me.

"No!" Texas and I cried together.

"No? I'm as good as Rosie. I raise my kids and I'm clean; although I get drunk occasionally, I try to keep myself neat and presentable. Fuck, I work hard, and then come here and cook and clean for you guys. And I know I'm a great person. Surely, I deserve the white picket fence, a nine-to-five man, and a happy family life with set vacations at certain times of the year?" Penny declared.

Each word stabbed deep into my heart.

"You do, but I'll never let you go," Texas said brokenly, and I saw that where I had intended to get through to Texas, Penny already had.

"We old ladies gave you guys everything and the treasure of your love we held so preciously you mistreated. Most of us didn't have a great life, but we opened ourselves up. And this is our thanks. Skanks rate above us. We don't deserve the goodness the princesses do. We are just clean cunts for you to dip in and know your brothers ain't fucked us. Great, now we realise our true value. Makes me wonder why we're with you." Penny spun on her heel and stormed out, and I ran a hand down my face.

"Whatever we say makes it worse," I moaned.

"It's time we sit down and look at why they're feeling like that," Mac declared. Out of all the brothers, he was the only one that the old ladies were talking to. And he was walking a fine line. Mac's loyalty was to us, but he disagreed with our decisions. I didn't envy Mac whatsoever.

Nods abounded. This whole scenario made them uncomfortable and forced them to deal with things they'd been blinkered to.

"For now, we have a brother to rescue," I replied.

Three hours later, I stood focused on the helicopter that had just lifted off with Calamity, Rosie, and Klutz on board. From what I'd seen, the kid was a mess. Barely alive. Below me moved those I called friends and brothers, and my heart ripped to see how many had come out to claim Calamity back. Because, to them, the boy mattered. It was slowly sinking in what we had thrown away. Calamity was another Axel, the club's heart, and we'd lost sight of that.

Texas was pale under his tan as he saw Phoe, Autumn, Artemis, and Lindsey below. Next to them were our missing brothers, prospects, and candidates. They'd all come for the boy, alongside Washington's, the Juno Group, Hawthorne's, and Delta Force. Even my eldest boy was down there. Those had been the ones to rescue our brother, not us. Rage had failed in more ways than one. We watched as they stacked bodies inside the clubhouse and rolled some drums in. Some fertiliser bags followed, and then the Delta Force guys moved around outside, planting something. Bombs, I guessed.

Phoe spat on the ground, followed by the other old ladies, and then proudly marched herself away. Harley and the others surrounded them as they escorted the women back to where the SUVs were. We'd discovered them and hidden our bikes elsewhere. I watched as James and Dylan stood speaking and moved out, too. Finally, everyone has left apart from Jacob. Like Phoe, he spat on the ground and then jogged away. Moments later, the clubhouse, bodies inside, and the smaller building, blew sky high.

"Time to leave. If Rage is caught here, we'll be under fire," Fish said, and I acknowledged.

I walked into the hospital they had taken Calamity to and discovered the missing Rage members. Blaze turned to me, clearly the group leader, and nodded. The other rescuers weren't present, but the old ladies were, and they were content sending us dirty looks. There was no sign of Rosie.

"What do you want?" Blaze sought.

"To know how Calamity is, we arrived too late to join the party," I replied.

"Surprised you bothered," Lindsey muttered, sending Lowrider a scorching glance.

"We fucked up, and we gotta fix this," I said

placatingly.

"How do you plan to fix this shit, Drake?" Rosie urged from behind.

She moved around us and stood next to Klutz.

"We'll make it right," I begged, and Rosie shook her head.

"Can you make Calamity's ten fingers work properly so he can paint fine detail again? They broke every single one of them. How about the two gaping holes in his palms, where they nailed train spikes through them? Calamity's hands will never regain his dexterity, and his design career is finished. Could you make that right? Stay!" Rosie snapped as she saw Texas move.

"Can you fix the flesh on his back where Clyde tore it from him? No? Okay, how about half his ribs being broken, his lung pierced and collapsed? Again, a no, Drake? And he might never ride again because they kneecapped Calamity, and docs don't know if they'll be able to repair the damage. Can you remove the two Lawless Rogue brands they burned so deep into Calamity's hips he'll feel their marks forever? Maybe you'll carry him everywhere because they caned his feet so badly he's got no skin left. Tell me how to solve that shit!" Rosie screamed as we all paled.

"Rosie, no…" Texas murmured.

"Texas, yes! Calamity's shoulder has shredded; he'll only have eighty per cent use of it. His leg and hip were dislocated for so long he'll have a permanent limp, whether or not they fix his knees. Calamity's kidney is so inflamed they've no choice but to take it out. He's also lost his appendix, which they beat to near bursting, and his spleen. I suppose plastic surgery will sort Calamity's broken bones in his face, but the bullet through his head? Could you fuckin' fix brain damage? Because if you can, I'll get on my knees and worship you like gods. They shot him. Docs says it's a million-to-one chance he will live. And if he does, what quality of life will Calamity have?"

I reeled as I heard the list of injuries the kid had suffered. Those fuckers shot him in the head. Would he survive?

"Calamity gave you everything, and you threw it back in his face, and you all have the bare audacity to crawl in here and say you made a mistake? God help me, if Calamity dies, watch your backs because I'll set out to make each of your lives a fuckin' misery. I'll take everything from you like you took from me. And all because Calamity loved me. You make me sick, all of you. I hate to look at you, and none of you are welcome here. If Calamity had his cut, they wouldn't have touched him. But a jealous, insecure asshole decided he didn't want his daughter dating a biker. So, fuck you all," Rosie finished, her chest heaving with emotion.

I stood there as Rosie's hatred washed over me. And I couldn't deny any of it because I had been the one to remove Calamity's cut. I'd gone with the vote instead of my gut. And I had known I was wrong.

"You thought I was throwing a tantrum when I mentioned you were all dead to me. That I'd come running back after a few weeks and forgive Texas and everybody else. That would never happen because Calamity is the very air I breathe. I can't live without him. There is no life without Calamity. He's my everything. And once you were his. But not anymore. So, I suggest you leave now because none of you are welcome," Rosie added and turned into Klutz's jacket.

Blaze stepped up.

"I'm glad you're here because it makes it less likely there'll be a scene. None of us are coming back. After what we've witnessed, our stomachs have turned. And today, it was those Calamity called friends who came for him. Where was Rage?" Blaze asked.

"We were there. We saw what happened," Apache said.

"Where was Rage when Calamity was kidnapped? You've ranted about a new Rage, an improved Rage, and there's little evidence. Rage came for Jett and me when we were taken and only prospects. Rage let a brother walk, even though his choosing Rosie over his cut told you something. But Rage fucked over the best they had, and Calamity has suffered plenty. Calamity and Rosie need their family around them. Whether we create an MC and become their family that way or just stay tight to them, we don't know. But Drake, we ain't coming back, not how it is," Blaze said, and those surrounding him nodded.

Even my own sons.

I couldn't meet Harley's direct gaze and Micah point blank refused to look at me. I instead instinctively sought my source of comfort. Except for today, there was nothing there but an empty shell. Phoe shook her head, unable or unwilling to give me what I needed.

"How many chances do you want? Drake, I've been here by your side, trying to show you the tyrants you were becoming, and you ignored everything. An innocent boy, one as close to me as my flesh and blood, lies fighting for his life. And should Calamity survive? What will he do, Drake? His hands are so fucked, his career is over. Calamity will never paint such beautiful art again.

And Rage took that from him like they stole his dignity, honour, respect, friendship, and family. Because you hate change Drake, you hate being confronted with shit you know shouldn't be accepted. And now that boy lies fighting for his life. I can't forgive that, no matter how much I love you," Phoe announced softly.

And maybe Phoe's words hurt the most because I understood they were spoken from a place of deep disappointment.

I quietly nodded my head and tilted my chin towards the door. Silently, Rage filed out.

"Don't bother coming back. I never want to see any of you again," Rosie shouted, and her verbal dagger hit me straight between the shoulders.

Fuck, I would fix this.

Chapter Nine.

Six weeks later.

Rosie

Calamity was now back in Rapid City. He'd
arrived three weeks ago after doc's Paul and Gibbons
said he was stable enough to travel. Calamity hadn't
yet regained consciousness and remained in a coma.
His fingers had healed, although there was some loss
of dexterity, and I'd hired the best physiotherapist to
work on my man. Hayleigh came daily, working on
moving his hands, stretching tight skin, and ensuring
muscles obeyed her. Hayleigh proclaimed that as
Calamity's fingers had been clean breaks, he would
regain ninety per cent use of them. But she needed to

keep the tendons moving, leaving them unattended would end his career.

Hayleigh also worked on his hips, knees, ankles, and feet. For Calamity's shoulder, she promised at least eight-five per cent usage, and she said he'd walk with a limp. In winter, Calamity would feel the cold in his left hip, but it was better than nothing. Doc Paul primarily took over Calamity's care after I argued with the other doctors. He'd learned of a new technique being used on burn victims and wished to try it on Calam's torn-up back. Dr Paul had told me about it as soon as he arrived at the hospital, and we had a doctor flying out hours later.

The procedure was called RECELL Autologous Cell Harvesting Device. And while I didn't understand it properly, it reduced pain and scarring and helped joint mobility. The procedure offered faster healing and improved traditional scarring left behind by skin grafts. The technique was for burn victims, but as Calamity had lost so much flesh, Doc Paul wanted to try it. Once Calamity's previous doctors refused, I overruled them and, with Doc Paul's help, flew in an expert.

Dr Fordman had collected a small skin sample from Calamity and soaked it in an enzyme solution to create a liquid. The new liquid had cells which played a major part in healing wounds. The solution was sprayed on the entirety of Calamity's back and would be repeated when needed. Dr Fordman was curious to see if it would work on Calamity, which was why he'd agreed to do the procedure. And blow me if it wasn't working. There was already far less scarring than expected.

Overjoyed at seeing the most vicious whip marks fading, I'd donated twenty million of Calamity's money to Dr Fordham's centre. Calamity would have done the same. Four weeks ago, once it was established Calamity was in a coma, Scott arrived and gave me power of attorney. Now I had legal rights over Calamity's care, rehabilitation, wealth, and companies. Scott and I had decided not to inform the three CEOs of what was happening as it was just such an upheaval.

This is why, despite some doctors telling me that Calamity was brain dead, I refused to believe them and kept Calamity's care to the highest standard. I was also perversely grateful that Calamity was unaware of what was happening around him. He'd undergone surgery on his face four times, the last only a few days ago, to correct his jaw. Calamity was nearly as perfect as he'd been before. Only a scar remained above his eye and one below his jawline near his ear. The bullet wound would be covered by his hair. How the bullet hadn't shattered Calamity's brain was a miracle I didn't question. We'd used the same surgeon Lindsey had gone to, to rebuild Calamity's face.

Hayleigh kept up his muscle strength while I searched for the best surgeons to put Calamity's battered body together again. One way or another, Calamity was coming back to me, and when he did, I didn't want him to view the wreck of his body.

Clyde and the other survivors had been dealt with and died in excruciating pain. Clyde took the longest to die. All the while being told he'd failed because Calamity lived and had the best care money could provide. I'd watched everything they'd suffered. Blaze and those that had left Rage had dished the revenge I chose and craved, and I'd remained in a chair observing as they received their just fate. Klutz had wanted me to stay apart from the gore and mess, but I couldn't.

I had to watch their justice and death for Calamity. And it soothed the part of me that screamed to hurt someone. Every stab, slash and inch of pain comforted the ugliness, finally allowing it to recede when Clyde passed last.

We'd also discovered how they'd found out about Calamity's inheritance.

When Mrs Travis's body was discovered, Clyde had tried turning the cop's eyes to Calamity. Clyde thought it a fine revenge to be locked up for the murder of the woman Calamity loved. Instead, the autopsy proved she'd died of a heart attack, as we knew. But there had been an obituary for Mrs Travis detailing who she was, and we'd been unaware. And when Scott went looking for Calamity, he'd obviously gone to Clyde's house. While Scott refused to divulge how much Calamity inherited, Clyde guessed millions.

Clyde and his club had searched for Calamity, finding him six months ago in Rage. Knowing they couldn't afford a war with Rage, they waited, and finally, Rage acted in Lawless Rogues' interests. By kicking Calamity, Rage exposed him to his father and MC. Something I could never forgive Rage for.

Over time, the old ladies had gone home, but they'd stayed away for a full month, making their point clearly. From what I heard, their relationships were poor, and there was a barrier between husband and wife. But Blaze and the others visited daily and remained loyal to their fallen brother. Jett had informed me that Drake was breaking his back to resolve their issues, and I told Blaze to go with his gut. I wouldn't hold a grudge against them if they returned to Rage. We'd still be family.

As for the vet clinic and rescue centre, both were being steadily built. I'd finally discovered a builder with a rep almost as good as BlackRock Construction, and both centres were now under construction. Everything was fine, apart from the fact Calamity needed to wake up and hear that he was going to be a dad. According to the doctor, I was two months pregnant, although, by my count, I was six weeks because I knew when I'd fallen. But they did it from the date of the last period, so eight weeks it was.

I'd told Calamity countless times, hoping he'd wake up and nothing. But I was sure he heard me somewhere because I was not accepting this brain dead bullshit. Calamity wasn't brain dead; he was recovering. Watch them get a bullet in the head and see how they recovered! A knock sounded, and I glanced up, and a new nurse entered. She smiled before preparing a syringe.

"What's that?" I asked, sitting up.

"Oh, it's a pain reliever," she answered. "Just place this in the IV, and he won't suffer anymore."

"Stop. I wasn't aware of a change in medication. Don't insert that needle until I confirm with a doctor!" I said, rising to my feet.

My gut was screaming something was wrong. The nurse sent that sideways grin again and flicked the top of the needle.

"Just a little prick into his IV. Billy won't feel a thing." She smirked.

No sooner had the words left her mouth than I tackled her. I'd no idea who this bitch was, but no one here called him, Calamity, Billy. She punched me, catching me off guard as she stumbled back to Calamity's IV. I spun and knocked her hand away, screaming for help, and the fake persona dropped. Hate blazed at me from angry eyes as she pulled a knife and slashed it at me.

"Stay the fuck away from him!" I screamed and yelled for security again.

The woman came at me, the needle raised to jab Calamity anywhere, and I smashed her in the head with a tray, and she stumbled backwards. A burning sensation hit my cheek as she did, but I used the tray again and whacked her. Footsteps bounded towards me as I plastered myself across Calamity's bed, protecting him from this whacked bitch.

"Who the fuck are you?" I hissed as she lay there, blinking.

The needle had jammed into her ribs. The bitch

must have landed on it when she fell.

"All you had to do was let him die," she spat, her eyes unfocused.

"You were trying to murder him," I yelled as blood splashed on the floor.

"I whelped the little bastard, and he couldn't even give us a few million," she hissed. There was venom in her voice, but it lacked strength.

"Deirdre, isn't it? Guess what? I killed your husband. Everything Clyde did to Calamity, I did to him twice over. And then I threw his body to the hogs. Ain't shit left of him," I whispered.

Hatred spun across Dierdre's face as she struggled, bleeding. The door finally flew open, and a nurse and doctor hurried in.

"What happened?" the nurse cried, kneeling next to Deirdre.

"Bitch tried to insert that needle into Calamity, but I'd not approved a medication change. She hit me, I whacked her with the tray, and she fell. Dierdre must have landed on the tip. She's Calamity's mother. She was trying to kill him," I yelled as security arrived, followed by a frantic Klutz. He took one look at me and started yelling for medical attention. On seeing Klutz, I began sliding to the floor. Klutz shoved past the nurse, bending over the woman's body, and caught me as my knees gave out.

"What's wrong?" I asked as burning pain flowed through my cheek.

"The bitch cut you open, Rosie; you need stitches!" Klutz yelled as the room started filling.

"Klutz, I'm pregnant," I hissed as my eyes closed.

"Got ya, babe," Klutz whispered, and I felt a kiss on my head.

Klutz was yelling, and I gave up, snuggled into his embrace, and drifted away.

I woke up in a bed next to Calamity's, confused and dazed at first. This was not ideal. My hand rose and touched a bandage covering my right cheek. Fuck, that bitch must have cut me deep. When I looked around, I realised we'd changed rooms.

I lay there, taking in what happened when the door opened, and Jett entered with Sin. On seeing me awake, they both hurried over.

"What the hell happened, Jett?" I demanded after fussing over Sin's baby belly.

"That was Dierdre Tomkins, Calamity's mother, and her pathetic attempt to claim his wealth. She had a second needle, Rosie, for you. If you hadn't picked up something was wrong, she'd have stabbed you the moment you turned your attention away."

I snorted in disgust at Jett's words.

"Yeah, I have a will. Everything goes to Klutz, Micah, you, Blaze, and Hunter. Scott and I wrote it a few weeks ago when I became power of attorney for Calamity. Jesus, this money is more trouble than it's worth," I replied.

Jett blinked at the revelation.

"Who else would I leave it to?" I demanded, and he shrugged. "Jett, you stayed by our sides the whole time. We love you as much as you do us."

"Klutz said you looked like a warrior princess. He mentioned you'd plastered yourself across the bed, stopping anyone from reaching Calamity. Gotta love you for that image," Jett teased, trying to ease the sudden tension in the room. Which meant Jett was uncomfortable with the declarations of love.

"After all Calamity's suffered, that cunt wasn't ending his life. What happened to her?" I demanded.

"The whore died from injecting herself by accident," Sin said with a grin.

"Oh, Karma is such a bitch!" I chuckled, amused.

Calamity

In the deepest, darkest recess of my mind, I heard a scream. One I recognised.

Rosie!

She was in trouble. I allowed myself a moment of weakness, not wanting to face the blinding pain of my body again, and swirled around in the thick, tar-like darkness. It was safe here. Nobody could reach or hurt me anymore, and I had my memories. I'd curled up like a cat, content to stay for a while. But that screech jolted me. And a flicker of my consciousness jumped awake. Slowly, I dragged myself to awareness. Rosie needed me. And I would not stay here licking my wounds.

Desperately shoving the awareness of impending

pain aside, I struggled to my feet and looked up at the long climb. I had to reach the tiny spark of bright light in the far distance above me. Shit, that was going to be hard. Shuffling, I took my first step and kept Rosie's beautiful face in mind and the fear behind her scream.

Rosie

I'd seen the surgeon who assured me he could remove the worst of the scar down my face when I was ready. To be honest, I wasn't that bothered by it. This was a badge of pride; I had got it by saving my man. I'd been discharged from the hospital five days now, after spending four days admitted, and was sitting with Calamity, reading to him. Calamity loved the Clive Cussler books, so weeks ago, I'd started reading them to him from the beginning. While I'd never read them before, I found myself soon caught up in the adventures of Dirk Pitt and Al Giordano.

Rage had not returned after I had Drake and Texas tossed from the hospital. But every day friends visited. Not just our former Rage family but people from Ali-kat's community, who remembered Calamity and the barn raisings he'd attended with fondness. Or someone from Washingtons. Calamity was a familiar face from hauling Rage women out of there. But we were never alone and were surrounded by love and friendship. Or a friend from the Juno

Group popped in.

Micah hovered so much that I sent him away. He was worrying himself sick and I knew he had a big job on. I called Chance, and forced Micah to return to work and we spoke several times a day on the phone. It wasn't perfect but it was better.

Penny ensured hot fresh food was dropped off for me every day. Whoever was visiting would stop and pick up a basket from the Reading Nook. The nurses on Calamity's ward were often grateful for the baked goods Penny sent their way. Penny had confided in me that although she'd returned home, things were not good between her and Texas. This worried me because I knew they truly loved each other. But Texas had shown his asshole ways in full strength, and Penny wasn't prepared to deal with them.

This morning Savage had come, the quiet man sitting silently as I read to Calamity. Much like Gauntlet, Savage hardly said anything. He just wanted to be present and show his support. None of the brothers coming wore their cuts, so I guess things were still unsettled at Rage. Not that I asked. It was nothing to do with me. Klutz had moved into my house to look after the animals and was apparently teaching Peter all the wrong words to say. I tried to get home a few times a week to give myself a break and a chance to recover my strength.

The nights I stayed home, someone remained on guard duty with Calamity. We'd not risk anyone getting close to him again. I was paying Hawthorne's and Juno Group to keep a twenty-four-hour man on

Calamity. Klutz knocked and stuck his head around with a sneaky grin.

"Lunch?" I asked, and he nodded. Only this time, he carried two baskets.

To my surprise, a pink nose peaked out of one, and I jumped, startled. Klutz drew the blinds and then put the basket on the bed. I giggled as the lid flipped open, and Empress crawled out. The little cat stalked up Calamity's body and curled next to his throat. Her rough little tongue flicked out, and Empress licked him before setting into a remarkably deep purr.

"Poor baby, wounded soldier. Precious is here," Precious cawed, stalking up the bed after daintily climbing out of the basket. She settled on the other side of Calamity's head and began grooming him. Calamity's head had been shaved when they removed the bullet from his brain, but it was growing back quickly. Finally, Klutz hauled Jester out, and the arctic fox curled up on Calamity's chest.

"You're going to get into so much trouble." I laughed, and Klutz shrugged.

"Calamity loves animals, and I know he can hear and sense us. I thought they might help," Klutz replied with a shrug.

Precious remained cooing at Calamity while Empress continued her loud purr. Jester just watched with bright eyes. Every so often, Precious rubbed her beak against Calamity's cheek and spoke to him.

"Wake up, sleeping beauty," she chided gently.

My heart broke because she bobbed her head up each time she said that to see if Calamity's eyes had opened. Poor Precious couldn't understand why Calamity was not giving her love.

For an hour, Klutz and I talked while the animals loved on Calamity. The miracle I had hoped for, that maybe Calamity's Precious or Empress might wake him, didn't happen. Disappointment formed, and I tried shoving it aside. At this rate, I'd have the baby before Calamity woke up.

"Have you thought of any names?" Klutz asked as he gently placed a hand on my stomach. At ten weeks, I had a very tiny bump, which Klutz loved to rub his big mitts all over. I didn't mind. It brought me some sense of closeness to Calamity.

"No, not a clue," I replied as the door opened and a nurse entered. She was smiling until she saw the animals.

"What on earth is happening?" she exclaimed loudly.

"Shhh, sleeping beauty is sleeping," Precious chastised, and the nurse's mouth dropped open. Empress popped her little head up, and Jester opened an eye. The noise didn't bother them because of living with Peter and the others.

"Thought they might help," Klutz admitted.

"That's a raven. You can't have that diseased creature in here! And is that a fox? Omg. Remove them now!" the nurse cried.

Doc Paul entered and stopped on the threshold.

"Someone like to explain?" he asked mildly, looking amused.

The nurse launched into a diatribe while Klutz and

I inserted our comments. When the nurse ran down, Precious eyed her with distaste.

"Wash your mouth out, bitch! This little lady has her bath every night. By the smell of you, you've not been doing your undies!"

My jaw dropped, and Klutz choked on a chuckle.

"Precious! That's so rude and unlike you!" I exclaimed.

"Smells like fish, fish in a whorehouse!" Precious cawed.

"Why you…"

"That is enough, nurse. Perhaps you should leave," Doc Paul said firmly.

"Here, fishy, fishy, fishy," Precious taunted, ruffling her feathers and rubbing her beak against Calamity's cheek.

"What have you been teaching her?" I demanded, spinning on Klutz, who was full-out laughing.

"Must have been Peter. Precious has absorbed some of his insults," Klutz howled as Precious settled back into grooming Calamity.

I shook my head in disbelief as Doc Paul stroked her head.

"Well, hello there," Precious flirted.

"Yes, indeed, hi," Doc Paul said with wonder.

Klutz made a choking noise and pointed. I followed his finger and saw a pair of blue eyes looking back at me.

"Hey, handsome, let me see those baby blues," Precious cawed.

Calamity's eyes moved sideways as Precious

walked down his shoulder and up his chest. Precious peered into his face as one side of his mouth tugged upwards.

"Well, I never!" uttered Doc Gibbons, entering the room with the irate nurse behind him. She stopped as she saw Precious and Calamity eyeing each other.

"He's brain dead," she exclaimed.

"Clearly not!" Klutz retorted as tears streamed down my cheeks.

Precious gave Calamity a peck on the cheek before moving away as Empress stretched and yawned before taking her place. Jester shoved Empress aside, and Calamity's lips curved into a bigger smile as Empress appeared between Jester's ears.

"Jes... ter!" Calamity spoke.

Doc Paul carefully lifted Jester and Empress to one side and began checking Calamity. Calamity's eyes kept mine with wonder, and he talked again.

"Ba... by."

"Yes, Calam, I'm pregnant," I sobbed as I launched towards him. I clutched his hand and held it to my cheek as Klutz stood and grabbed Calamity's feet.

"Bro... ther. Kept... safe," Calamity stuttered.

Klutz nodded.

"We looked after Rosie. You rest now. We've got you back. Nothing else fuckin' matters apart from that!" Klutz said. His usually firm voice had a wobble in it.

Calamity winked tiredly and then closed his eyes.

I yanked out my phone and dialled Micah.

As soon as the news broke that Calamity was awake, anyone and everyone turned up. Jett and Hunter were first, with Blaze on their heels. They paused in amazement at seeing the three animals curled around Calamity. Doc Paul had argued with the ward and managers. He loudly explained that Calamity had been diagnosed as brain dead, yet when the animals were introduced, he woke up. Finally, alongside Doc Paul and Gibbon's arguments, a five-million-dollar donation had convinced the higher-ups to let them stay.

So when Blaze, Jett, and Hunter arrived, seeing Jester, Empress and Precious was a bit of a shock. Especially when Precious got chatty and charmed them. Empress had allowed Jester to curl up against Calamity's throat, and she was laid between his ears, observing anyone who went near her human. Precious was talking Blaze's ear off, and he looked totally taken by her when Savage and Gauntlet entered. On their heels came Slate, Harley, Wild, and Cowboy. The room was crowded when Sin, Mina, Ali-kat, and Aurora Victoria rolled in with Penny. Micah was last to arrive but shoved his way to the side of the bed. Everyone watched the bed for any sign of life from Calamity.

"Wake up, beauty boy," Precious cawed in his ear.

"Beauty boy, I'm not gonna let that fucker live it down." Blaze laughed.

Precious sent him a dirty look, and he stopped.

"Aw, pretty girl, I wasn't laughing at you," Blaze said, trailing a finger down her back.

"I'll shit on you," Precious warned, and I cried with laughter. Precious had definitely absorbed some of Peter. Everyone else roared at the shock on Blaze's face. Micah choked as happy blue eyes watched us from the bed.

"There it is. The bird keeps Calamity awake," Doc Paul said to a colleague who'd squeezed into the room. Both men were shaking their heads in amazement.

"Kiss," Calamity croaked.

Precious bent her head and rubbed her beak against his lips.

"Precious wake beauty boy. Beauty woke. Precious is clever. He's a numb nut," she cawed and looked at Blaze.

"You'll have to bribe her to like you again," I said. "She loves oranges."

Blaze nodded, making a mental note.

"Do you know who you are?" Doc Paul urged, moving forward through the crush. Another doctor appeared, and the three of them stood around his bed.

"Cal... am... ity."

"Well done, and the year?"

"Two... zero... two... zero."

"Twenty-twenty, good man," Doc Paul praised.

"Do you recognise these people?" the second guy asked.

"Ros... ba... by."

"Yes, Rosie is pregnant. Congrats, you're going to

be a father," Doc Paul responded with a smile.

Calamity turned his head towards Klutz, Micah, Blaze and the men standing there.

"Broth... ers. Mine. Fam... ily."

"Calamity's fully aware, apart from his speech, there doesn't seem to be any damage," the third doctor said, sounding awed.

"There'll be more rigorous testing, but Calamity at the moment seems fine, Rosie. Do not push him too much or let Calamity overextend himself. He can have sips of water, which probably isn't helping his speech, having such a dry throat. Answer what he wants within moderation. I don't want to trigger a relapse," Doc Paul said ten minutes later after Calamity was asked many questions.

I nodded.

"And keep the party down, please. And after today, only four guests per visit," the second doctor spoke.

He smiled at Calamity.

"Young man, I declared you brain dead myself. I have never witnessed such a miracle, heard of rare ones, but never believed to be present for one. You've given me faith," the guy said before leaving the room.

The other doctors followed him out and huddled in a crowd outside. I wasn't interested in them. The only thing I was engrossed in was Calamity's face and how it lit up when he saw everyone around him. Calamity hadn't lost his family; they were there in force for him.

Chapter Ten.

Calamity

"How are you feeling, bro?" Klutz asked as he sat down.

I was glowering out of the French doors, so surely that was a clue.

"Truthfully? I'm screwed, dude. Can't hold a pencil, can't hold a knife and fork, can't fuckin' walk. I'm pissed off and useless. Hayleigh did a great job of not letting my muscles waste, but if they won't obey me, what's the damn point? Nothing works as it's meant to!" I erupted, and Klutz sat back with a nod. Five days had passed since I'd woke from the coma and a day since I'd arrived home.

"At least the stammers are gone," Klutz quipped, and I glowered even more.

"Yeah, I can get a phone sales job," I bitched.

"Calamity, you're alive. That's the main thing, you might disbelieve it, but we all fuckin' do. Rosie went through hell those twenty-four hours you were taken and then spent weeks at your bedside praying for you to wake up. Know it's gotta hurt being back to square one, but believe me, that girl is happy as long as you are breathing," Klutz said firmly.

Yeah, but I was worthless to Rosie now. Shit, I couldn't even cut my food up. Rosie had to do it as my muscles spasmed and refused to grip when I needed them. Rosie was feeding me, which was a further insult. Yeah, I wasn't the man she'd fallen in love with, and I had begun to believe I'd never be self-sufficient again. Rosie did not deserve to be stuck with me. Bitterness was welling deep inside, and I recognised the emotion but could not stop it from growing.

"Rosie deserves better," I mumbled and moved my eyes away from Klutz's perceptive gaze.

"Yeah, she does. Rosie always did, but she chose you. Now you gonna grow up or lose that girl to somebody who'd walk through fire for her? Once, I thought you were that guy. But all this sulking and pouting, it's been five days Calamity, five freaking days. Nobody expects a miracle except you. So what if you can't grasp a knife and fork? You can fucking grip a large item. The pressure you're putting on yourself is what's holding you back. If you truly love Rosie, then man the fuck up!" Klutz said and climbed to his feet. Klutz sent me a stare of disgust.

"Calamity, you rose out of the dirt like a phoenix in

full rebirth. Stayed true to your personality and morals and ignored those who would tear you down. For eighteen years, you battled the evil in your life and found something worth living for. Then motherfuckers tore that away. But you have a stunningly beautiful girlfriend and a child. Find that strength you once had because if you fuck up, Clyde and Dierdre win. And they always will, going forward. You might not have the body strength you had before, nor the fine motor skills, but that is not what made you special.

"It was your heart, Calamity, that drew people to you, the hope and belief in a good life, a better future. Everyone wanted to be near you because of that inner light. Clyde tried to beat that out of you. Are you telling me Clyde won and killed that uniqueness? A group of men and women banded together to rescue you, bro, because of your specialness. Calamity, I lost my career, one I loved and hoped to excel at. And I discovered something else that can make me happy. Choose, Calamity, to live or wallow in selfish grief and misery. And lose everything you have left."

Fuck, that was harsh.

Klutz left, leaving me to think. What an asshole to land that shit on me when I was hurting. But a small niggle worried me. Was Klutz right? Everybody kept telling me this was temporary, and Hayleigh was one of the best in her field. Hayleigh knew what she was saying and doing. But dare I hope because every time I think I have something good, something takes it away from me? Damn, I was spiralling into depression.

My mind was scattered. Even now, I remembered little of Clyde and Lawless Rogue's brutality. Certain aspects stuck out, the breaking of my fingers, the kneecapping, those mattered because I wanted to paint and ride. I could recall them in implicit detail because they took away something that meant everything to me. A scream was lodged in my throat and was fighting for release.

During my torture, I'd screamed, roared, and cried out with pain, but this was a different cry. This was against the injustice I had suffered, and the question kept running through my head, why me? I'd done everything possible to be a good person, yet shit continued hitting me. Shit didn't stop; even at Rage, I'd been beaten and shot. Why me? What was so wrong with me? Crap never stopped happening, and I grabbed a lamp and hurled it at the French doors. The glass shattered and the scream I'd locked away broke free. I slid to the floor, an emotional mess as sobs tore from my throat.

Rosie

"What were you thinking?" I ripped into Klutz as he entered the kitchen, where Hayleigh and I were standing.

"Need to lance that poison. If Calamity keeps that inside, it will destroy him. I pushed for a reason, and he needed that," Klutz said.

"Is that the doctor speaking?" I demanded furiously, not assuaged at all.

"Yes. Think I don't recognise mental trauma? Calamity is holding himself back. As soon as he lets go, he'll heal properly. But deep down, Calamity is that little boy asking why me? Calamity, the adult, knows life happens, but the kid inside doesn't. And I'm telling you, Rosie, if this doesn't release the poison, then I'll push harder," Klutz said.

I bristled at his tone because I didn't like it. Angry, I turned away from Klutz and began making sandwiches for lunch. Five minutes later, a crash echoed, and a scream ripped through the house. Frightened, I froze for several moments, heart pounding at the agony in Calamity's howl. Then I rushed towards the living room.

"No!" Klutz interrupted my mad dash, and Hayleigh reinforced him.

"Calamity needs me," I whispered.

"Not yet. Let him get it out, Rosie, and then go to him," Hayleigh said gently.

I paced back and forth as screams and choked sobs echoed, and it tore me apart not to be able to get to Calamity. As soon as the screaming stopped, Klutz stepped aside, and I rushed past him. The scene that confronted me gave me pause. The French doors were smashed. Calamity sat on the floor with Henrik. His arms were wrapped around the big dog, and Calamity sobbed into his fur. Henrik was pushed firmly against Calamity, offering silent comfort.

I raced forward as Calamity lifted his head, and I curled into his lap. Henrik gave us both a lick and then lumbered away. To my surprise, Jester, Precious, and Empress were lurking close to Calamity on the sofa.

"Okay now?" I asked, wiping the tears from his face.

Calamity snorted.

"Gonna be awhile till I'm fine, Rosie. But am I feeling better? Yeah. I'd bottled so much up. Shit, I think I might need therapy," Calamity admitted, and my eyes widened.

"If that's what you want, then we'll arrange it," I agreed.

"Think I'll have that if I'm to be any use to you and the baby. Can't have these doubts and thoughts rattling around and growing. They'll tear me apart, Rosie. And ruin what I have with you. And for our future, I'll go to hell and back," Calamity said, and a sob rose in my throat.

"Love you," I whispered.

"Not as much, babe, as I love and worship you."

Calamity

I'd called Blaze, Gauntlet, and Cowboy to come to our house. It had been a week since my breakdown, and I'd seen a therapist twice. That shit felt awkward, opening up to a stranger, but it was also cathartic.

Today I was planning to expel another demon. My brothers needed their brothers. This crap with the split in Rage needed ending. Rosie informed me that the old ladies were rarely in Rage, even though they were living back with their husbands. They used the Reading Nook to meet up, driving the Rage men insane. I planned to bring about amends.

"What's up?" Blaze asked once they'd settled.

"It's time for you all to return home. Too late for Klutz and me because we handed in our cuts officially. You guys didn't. Words were exchanged, but the formal handing over of the cuts hasn't happened. I need you to breach the rift between the old and new brothers and heal Rage. That would help me," I said honestly.

Blaze instantly baulked. His jaw jutted out, and his arms crossed.

"We decided to stand by you. That hasn't changed."

"Not saying it has, but you can still be part of Rage and my brother. I want everyone to heal, and nobody's gonna heal separately. You and Rage need each other," I said calmly.

Gauntlet glowered. "Calamity, I needed a family who stuck by each other through thick and thin. What I received were two sides which have totally different ideas about where the MC was heading. What would happen if I fell for Jodie or Serenity? Obviously, I'd have the same fate as you. Those princesses are gonna look for a strong man, and if he's a biker, then it's their decision. Don't want a noose around my neck if I fall in love with the wrong person."

"Gauntlet, I get that. But tell Drake that. I know Rage has dug a big hole, but they'll eventually listen. Trust in Drake and the processes," I urged.

"It's the fuckin' processes that are bad," Cowboy snapped.

"Then tell Drake, inform him what's wrong, or he'll not see it and carry on thinking he's correct. I'm just asking you to consider making things right. Hell, I can't force you," I said.

"We'll discuss and think about it, but no matter what happens, we will always be brothers, and Rage will not come between that," Gauntlet replied.

"And that's all I seek, brother." I smiled.

Progress had been made. Possibly not enough, but baby steps were okay.

Rosie

"Calamity, I'm going to take a walk to the rescue centre and check the progress. Do you want to come?" I called out.

"No, babe, I'm working with Hayleigh. Go ahead," Calamity yelled back.

A smile crossed my lips. Ever since the breakdown, Calamity had stopped fighting and was cooperating with Hayleigh, and it showed. He could now hold a knife and fork and cut and eat his meat. He could also stand longer and participated in the exercises with enthusiasm instead of a have-to attitude. Calamity still had memory gaps, and sometimes, while he knew the answer to something, he couldn't articulate it. But considering the other crueller options, I'd take that any day.

"Be back in an hour," I called out, and Henrik barked.

Since Calamity had cried, Henrik had decided Calamity was his person, which completely put Layla out. It was funny watching the two fight over who got closest to Calamity while Jester, Precious, and Empress sat on his lap.

I stepped over Terence, who was chasing Harold, while Fanny watched from a corner. She had nearly given Klutz a heart attack when she first keeled over, and it had been a moment of pure enjoyment. The poor man had begged me to help while massaging her ribs. When Fanny popped back up, and I explained what she was, Klutz had not been amused. Of course, Calamity and I were.

I left the house and strolled down the drive. It was not a long walk but one I demanded. Just as Calamity needed to clear the cobwebs sometimes, so did I. I noticed Savage pulling into the new clinic and diverted my path there. Seeing Savage was a surprise, and I wondered what was happening.

"Savage!" I shouted, and he raised a hand as he dismounted the bike.

"Yo, Rosie," Savage called as I approached.

"What are you doing?"

"Saw you and thought I'd check you're okay. So I stopped before going to the house," Savage replied.

"Oh no, sorry, I'm walking to the rescue centre to check how the build was going. The clinic is almost done."

Savage frowned as he glanced over.

"The car belongs to one of the builders, then?"

What car? I turned and spied a rust bucket parked by the entrance.

"Nobody should be here today," I said, moving towards the building's door. Savage fell into step beside me, his watchful gaze casting wary glances around us.

To my surprise, the door was open, and I pushed in, wondering what the hell was happening.

"Hello?" I called and wrinkled my nose. I could smell gasoline. What on earth was going on? There was a shuffling noise behind the counter in the hallway, which led to the offices and examination rooms.

Savage held a finger to his lips and moved quietly towards the entrance. The scent of petrol got stronger.

"Stay where you are, or I drop this," a man yelled as Savage and I entered. I stared in shock at Brett. He didn't look so impeccable now. Brett's clothes were creased, his hair greasy and lank, and he'd a wild expression.

"What the fuck are you doing?" Savage demanded as Brett held a lighter up.

"Bitch burned my world. I'm going to set Rosie's on fire," Brett snarled.

I saw two gasoline cans by his feet.

"Leave it. If this burns down, I can rebuild," I said,

tugging on Savage's cut.

Savage raised his gun, keeping an aim on Brett.

"Ain't the point, Rosie. This guy sexually assaults you and then tries to burn your clinic down? Think we're the type of guys to let sick shit slide? Asshole's card was already marked because of the assault. No chance I'm letting him do this," Savage growled.

"This doesn't matter. Hell, the equipment isn't even installed. This is just a shell, Savage," I begged.

Brett had a look in his eye that told me he wasn't operating on all cylinders.

"Fuck," Savage muttered.

A squeal left my lips as someone grabbed me from behind and placed a stranglehold around my neck. I fought and then stopped as a gun was put against my temple. Savage backed against the wall, aiming at both Brett and my attacker.

"Hello again, bitch. Remember me?" Rex growled into my ear, and I stiffened.

What the hell?

"Rex!"

"Yeah, just little ole me. Your biker boyfriend fucked me up and ruined my life, and I've been planning revenge for years. Wonder how he's gonna take to losing you?" Rex snarled, and I tried to turn my head from the fetid breath wafting in my face.

"Calamity will kill you," I retorted. "You should have stayed away."

"That motherfucker ain't doing shit. He's been broken and battered. Now he knows what it's like. And soon, he'll understand what it feels like to lose everything. We are gonna have some fun, Brett and I, with you. And when we're done, we might just kill you. Or maybe leave you damaged in the dirt," Rex muttered.

Savage snarled as Brett moved.

"One more step, and I will put a bullet in you," Savage growled.

"Drop my main man there, and I'll shoot Rosie right now in front of you," Rex snapped as Brett kept coming.

"Savage shoot!" I cried. Nope, I wasn't cooperating with either sexual predator.

"Rosie," Savage said as he nodded. Savage was trying to send me a message as Brett reached my side and grinned. He flicked the lighter at Savage, who dived to one side as Rex hauled me into the reception area. There was a whoosh from the hallway, and I screamed Savage's name.

Rex was laughing as he and Brett dragged me outside, and a gunshot echoed. I elbowed Rex in the gut and dropped into a ball as a second shot resounded.

I glanced up and spotted Calamity and Hayleigh standing there. Brett's screams pierced the air as Calamity dropped his arm.

"Rosie, come here, baby," Calamity whispered as Hayleigh kept her gun trained on the two men. I didn't hesitate and scrambled across the ground. Calamity was sinking to his knees as I flung myself into his arms.

"My aim was off. Crap, I was aiming for his head,"

Calamity muttered. He'd hit Brett in the shoulder. Rex, however, was staring sightlessly at the sky. Hayleigh's shot had taken him straight in the middle of his heart.

"Savage is inside. He was standing in gasoline, and they threw a lighter," I sobbed as I watched smoke billow from my building. Calamity struggled to his feet when Savage rushed out of the entrance, coughing and choking.

"Fire's out. The suppression system's kicked straight in," Savage choked out and collapsed on his back. Hayleigh was tying Brett up and giving him an occasional kick as she did so. Brett was wailing and spouting shit, so she shoved a handkerchief in his mouth. A small giggle escaped me at the look on Brett's face. He was completely beside himself. Once Brett was secured, Hayleigh bent over, checked Rex for a pulse, and then hurried over to Savage, where she began checking his stats.

"How did you know?" I whispered as Calamity collapsed onto his butt. I burrowed in deeper.

"Savage sent a text that the door was open and to call for help," Calamity replied.

"I didn't see Savage do that," I responded.

"No worries, Rosie. He did it, and that was all that mattered. Although my fuckin' aim is off. I seriously did target Brett's head," Calamity complained.

I laughed. Only Calam would be miffed at missing getting a head shot.

"I've called the police. They're on their way," Hayleigh stated, and Calamity scowled.

"Not how we'd have dealt with it," Savage coughed.

"Well, it's the way I have. Suck it up," Hayleigh muttered, and Savage took on his usual glower.

"What a mess." I sighed.

"Can't believe Brett came after you. Why now? And is that the asshole from college I beat down?" Calamity asked, leaning forward and peering at Rex.

"Yeah. God only knows how those two ended up together," I replied. I watched as thoughts raced across Calamity's face.

"Bet Brett sought Rex out, looking for something to pin on you to force you to pull the lawsuit. Heard anything from your old clinic?

"Customers are leaving in droves, as Brett got bail posted by his aunt. Plus his work had got sloppy. But I'd not paid much attention because of what was happening to you. It would make sense that Brett would come after me if his income were affected. Plus, the rejection. That was plenty to fill Brett with vinegar and piss. But add to the fact he was caught outright lying, and his reputation was shredded, all that caused him to tip over the edge." Somehow, I knew I was right. Brett kept up screaming through the gag, but we ignored him. By the time sirens wailed down the drive, we'd all had enough of him.

Calamity

The fear lodged in my throat when Savage's

message came through and panic set in. As I tried to consider my options, Hayleigh came across as I told her what Savage had said. Before I knew it, I was bundled into her car, and we drove to the clinic. The journey took seconds, and Hayleigh and I waited outside with our guns ready. My hand and arm were shaking through stress, and the pressure was immense. When I saw Rosie being dragged out, I aimed and fired instantly. Rosie had training and knew to drop when a gunshot sounded, and she did beautifully. My stunning girl dropped to the ground as Hayleigh fired and hit the second attacker straight through the heart.

To my surprise, it was a beautiful shot and bang on target. Hayleigh kept Brett covered. Yeah, I recognised that asshole as Rosie scrambled towards me. My legs went weak in relief, and I bent down and hauled her close. Thank fuck, I thought as my arms wrapped around her. My woman and baby were safe. A frisson of fear ran down my spine as Rosie cried out that Savage was inside, which was quickly dispelled when he rolled out.

To claim I was astounded when I recognised Rosie's old college stalker was an understatement. I was more amused by Brett rolling around in the dirt and screaming through a gag Hayleigh had shoved in his mouth. Savage and I exchanged a look as Brett was finally hauled away by the cops. No doubt he'd get out again and come after Rosie. Next time we'd drop him where he stood. I couldn't understand Brett's obsession with her. Surely my girl wasn't the only one who'd ever told him no. The ego on the motherfucking asshole was beyond my understanding.

As soon as we were released after giving statements, I took Rosie home and headed straight for a bath. I stank from my workout, and Rosie needed a warm bath for comfort. I could turn the taps on now and run it while Rosie undressed. I loved this bath. Rosie hadn't stinted when she'd had the bathroom redone. The bathtub was a comfortable size for two, even with my height. Liberally, I sprinkled in Rosie's rose bubble bath and, once stripped, climbed in happily.

I stared unabashedly as Rosie entered naked and radiant. Her tiny baby bump was more noticeable now, and her skin glowed healthily. My cock twitched, and I looked down, surprised. It had been acting rather lacklustre lately, but clearly, Rosie like this triggered it. Rosie watched as I stroked my shaft as it grew in my hands. With a low growl, she knocked my hand aside and lowered herself into the bath, straddling me. Oh, now I came fully awake.

It was like a fish to water, red to a rose. As soon as my cock touched the outer walls of her pussy, I was desperate. Rosie smiled cockily as she took my mouth in a kiss, and I slid a hand between us and flicked her nub. Two could play her game. Rosie squirmed as I found the sweet spot her folds hid and began teasing her mercilessly. She responded by sucking my throat, which she knew turned me the fuck on. It had been months since I had been inside my woman, and I was impatient.

Rosie, however, seemed to want to play and while I'd usually indulge her, not tonight. I grasped her hips, shifted her into position, and fed myself into her. Fuckin' heaven, sheer unadulterated bliss. Rosie's tight walls gripped my cock as I slid in, making my head spin with the feel of her. Her little pussy welcomed me home as I sat upright in a surge of water and clasped her tightly to me.

I thrust inside, and Rosie responded, her lips parted and eyes warm and loving. She looked the epitome of Venus, made for loving. Droplets of water ran down her body, and my tongue flicked out to lick them. My cock pushed deeper, picking up the pace between us as I watched the satisfaction roll over Rosie's face. No matter what happened to me, I'd never forget how she looked right now. All woman and sensual pleasure. Rosie rolled her hips the way she knew I loved, and a gasp left my mouth as a wicked little smile crossed her mouth.

In payback, I shoved deeper, and Rosie threw her head back as a cry escaped her. My cock felt like it was going to break. I was so damn hard as I sought my release deep inside my woman. With a guttural groan, I came with such force I grew lightheaded. But not dazed enough that I didn't hold on to Rosie as she pursued her release, grinding against me. I poked a finger between us and flicked her nub, and Rosie let out a loud scream as she stiffened and then moved frantically.

I was a smug bastard when Rosie collapsed against

my chest. As far as I was concerned, only I would ever see the beauty of my woman in the throes of passion. Possessive as fuck it might be. Who the hell cared? Rosie and I were soulmates, and nothing could come between us. Not Clyde, Dierdre, Rex, Brett, or even her father. We were tied together for eternity; that was just how I liked it.

Chapter Eleven.

Rosie

Thanks to Savage dousing the fire as best as possible and the suppression systems kicking straight in, the damage wasn't as bad. Nando called and informed me that Brett was now being held without bail. That was a relief, though it appeared to annoy the hell out of Calamity. His physio was coming along well. He could walk longer, and while his hip hurt, Calamity refused to give in to it. Hayleigh declared his shoulder had reached full potential, which gave Calamity about the eighty-five per cent movement that had initially been suggested.

The only thing getting to him was his fingers. Calamity had gained enough dexterity to work on bikes and do normal everyday things. But his hand and eye communication were disjointed. Calamity was also frustrated by not being able to draw to his exacting standards. The one picture he drew ended up ripped to shreds as Calamity threw a tantrum. In honesty, it had been mediocre, but he was learning anew.

Two weeks had passed since the fire, and yesterday trucks arrived, bringing all the equipment we'd ordered. They'd been arriving from six in the morning and didn't stop until nine at night. Klutz and I, who'd been on site, had been exhausted organising the examination rooms. Meanwhile, Winnie had her hands full sorting the reception area. After a late dinner of pizza, we collapsed, happy but tired.

On Monday, the clinic would be open, and the week after, the rescue centre would have its grand opening. We were researching building the sanctuary and a re-homing shelter where no healthy animal would be euthanised.

Calamity really didn't care what I did with his money, which threw me because he'd grown up so poor. Sometimes I expected Calamity to say no and cling to it, fearful of losing the stability it offered. But no, he kept making suggestions and throwing cash at me. Calamity had noticed the land behind me had come up for sale, and he'd already bought it and had put in an offer for another large plot. That one had caused intense discussions.

Calamity wanted to open a place for boys and girls from disadvantaged areas who grew up like him but couldn't settle in a foster house. These kids, Calamity believed, were often tossed aside. He wished to build a proper home so they could each have a bedroom, a small bathroom, and their own living room. Calamity desired at least fifty suites and preferably one hundred. And he wanted to ensure they got their education, and after finishing school, they would find work. That was the sticking point between Calamity and me. Calamity demanded to contact Rage and see if they would take his kids as apprentices. Obviously, they could help around the clinic, sanctuary, rescue centre, and re-homing shelter.

But I didn't want Rage anywhere near us. It was fair to say I completely blamed them for what happened to Calamity while, as usual, he was the better person and more forgiving. In an attempt to divert Calamity from Rage, I suggested asking the old ladies and Hellfire or one of the other MCs. He said he'd consider it, but Rage was the local MC. We let the point drop, unwilling to argue it further.

Although he didn't say, I felt Calamity had latched onto the idea of a home for children because he thought his design career was over. Hayleigh assured me it was not, but Calamity was trying to rush that one aspect of his life. She had full confidence he would regain his skill. Maybe not completely, but close enough. My heart broke for how lost Calamity seemed sometimes. Calamity was used to being always surrounded by brothers because he'd lived at the clubhouse. It had been months since he had last seen it, or Rage, and I know he had a big hole inside him.

Calamity became obsessed with healing the rift

between Blaze and the now uncut brothers and Rage. He'd conducted several meetings to try to talk Blaze and the gang around, and it wasn't happening. They were still full of resentment, and it sucked. And I also knew that the old ladies remained spending their evenings together at the Reading Nook, and Phoe refused point blank to set foot on Rage. People were hurting, and that upset my kind-hearted man.

I stared off my porch into the lowering sun and turned my mind to another thing that bothered me. The dog fighting ring hadn't yet been shut down. Nando was working hard on it, but every time he discovered a lead, it was always after the fights had happened. He was no closer to learning who organised it or where the next one would be. Claiming Nando was frustrated was a vast understatement. Over twenty more dogs had been found dead, and I hated it. Wickedly, I longed to put those men in the ring and force them to fight to the death. See how they liked it.

I'd stayed in liaison with other vets, but no canines had been brought in that survived. One vet mentioned having four dogs taken in over a week by different people, but sadly, they died from their wounds. Rage was working on the problem, too, because Nando informed me, but they stayed away from me. Clearly, the organiser realised the RCPD and Rage were after him because the ring kept things tight to their chest.

I was three months pregnant, and it sucked because I hadn't told Texas. Calamity didn't push me to but made sure I understood I had his support if I did. I guessed how excited Texas would be to have a grandchild, but that baby wouldn't exist without Calamity. And Texas still hadn't acknowledged being wrong to vote Calamity from the club. I loathed how easily Calamity found it to forgive, while I longed to rant and rave.

Penny noticed, and I imagined she had informed Texas, but he hadn't contacted me. So be it. If Texas was waiting for me to contact him, he had a long wait ahead of him.

Micah came around every couple of days, finally being reassured Calamity was healing. The poor guy had run himself ragged with Klutz at first, wanting to do everything for Calamity but Hayleigh had read them both the riot act. Now they were much calmer around him, assured their friend was not going to die. Everything was as it was supposed to be.

Calamity

"Hello?" Drake asked, sounding confused.

"It's Calamity."

"Is everything okay?" Drake demanded, and I heard movement around him.

"Yeah, shit's fine. I'm calling about Blaze and the others," I announced.

"That's club business," Drake slowly replied.

"Don't worry, I get it. I ain't Rage anymore. But I was phoning to see if I could help repair the relationship between you. But seems you haven't learnt your lessons, Drake," I retorted. Drake drew in a deep breath, and I cut him off.

"This outsider will stop worrying about how to get his former brothers and his brothers back together. If you've still got this shitty attitude after everything that's happened the last few months, no wonder Blaze won't return. Rage has lost some damn good men, Drake, and I pity you."

Drake wheezed as I spat my last three words. Those hit home. I disconnected the call and sighed. Why would they have learned anything? Rage thought and truly believed they were above all. So let Rage get on with it.

Fuck the lot of them.

Two days later, my phone rang, and upon answering, I was surprised to hear Drake asking me not to hang up.

"What do you want?" I asked wearily.

"Got a lead on a dog fight. We're going to need a vet."

"I see. I'll ask her, but I can't promise Rosie will. Rosie really has an issue with you," I replied.

Drake made a sad noise, but I hardened my heart. I'd reached out two days ago and had been knocked back.

"And I'll tell you something. If Rosie comes, she'll not want to be harassed. Rage made your decision, and you were warned of the consequences. Now you suffer them," I added firmly.

"Heard Rosie's expecting," Drake expressed in a low voice.

"Yes, she is. And make no mistake, I'll protect Rosie with my life. Nobody will harass or say anything to hurt her if she agrees to attend. I'll be with her anyway, and Klutz, but no one approaches to give her the guilt trip. Because Rosie doesn't feel any regret," I replied.

I could almost hear Drake's brain ticking over.

"Agreed."

"Good, because mess with my girl, and I'll fuck up whoever is the culprit. I may be a cripple, but I can still fire a fuckin' gun," I cautioned.

Drake hissed as I said the word cripple. God knows why. It was clear I didn't matter.

"No one will mess with any of you," Drake promised.

"Be certain of that," I warned, and I hung up on him for the second time.

Rosie

Klutz stood by my side. In fact, he was plastered to it. We both carried medical bags as we stared at the barn in the distance that Drake swore had a dog fight being held tonight. Calamity was next to my SUV, talking to Blaze and Drake. Calamity kept pointing and shrugging and then shook his head and walked away.

"Drake swears the intel is correct, but it's ten at night, and people would have begun to arrive now. Blaze and Jett are sneaking down to see what they can discover. Got a bad feeling about this and believe Drake was given the wrong info," he said as he wrapped an arm around my waist and touched our baby. Happily, I smiled as I placed my hand over his.

"Something is off. There'd be people and vehicles present if a fight was happening," I agreed. Several of Rage watched us, including Texas, Axel, Ace, and Lex. I turned my gaze away from them and cupped Calamity's face.

"You okay?" he asked, peering down at me.

"Yeah, of course, don't worry about me. Just be careful out there," I replied.

Calamity's lips tightened and then softened as the realisation I wasn't saying that because he'd been hurt. I would have said that anyway. Calamity nodded and dropped a kiss on my head before rubbing the baby. We waited nearly ten minutes before Jett hollered at us to come down. Both Klutz and I were frowning.

"Need Klutz and Rosie!" Blaze bellowed, and we sped up. As we approached the barn we'd been watching, Calamity and Klutz drew weapons, but nobody attacked from out of the darkness. We hurried inside, and I flinched at the familiar smell of gasoline.

"Fuck!" I swore as I shook.

"Shit's safe for now. Motherfuckers tried to start a fire to cover shit up, but it failed to catch. Rosie, we

211

got five dogs still alive. You and Klutz need to get to them," Blaze replied.

"Rosie's not going inside. A single spark could send that up in smoke. Savage, could you run and get the SUV while the rest of us will bring the wounded out? Somebody needs to call Nando because we have a live-fighting scene. This can only be twenty-four hours old," Calamity spoke as he helped me away from the barn.

"Over here, baby, where if that thing blows, you're safe. Bring the dogs here," Calamity yelled as I began sorting through my bag for items I might need.

Klutz did the same opposite me.

"Hey," I mumbled. Klutz looked up, concern on his face. "Do as I say. If unsure, ask. Don't be afraid because I'm right here by your side. We'll save what we can," I reassured him. Klutz nodded, his dark expression turned tense.

Blaze and Jett appeared in front of us with two dogs in their arms. Both were badly wounded and Dobermans. Klutz and I worked together; the only words spoken were my commands to Klutz. His dog wasn't as bad off as mine, so as soon as I considered it stable, I asked Savage to put it in a cage for transport. As I acted on another, an American Pit Bull Terrier was brought out, and I sighed. Sadly, I doubted it would make it. Klutz worked hard on him while I finally handed over my Doberman and judged the next couple.

One was a Border Collie, and I could see blood bubbling from its mouth, while the second was a

Boerboel in terrible shape. Out of the two, the Boerboel stood the best chance. With a regretful look at the Border Collie, I launched into saving the Boerboel.

"What can I do?" Drake asked, and I shook my head as tears fell while I watched the Border Collie struggle for breath. Klutz moved, taking me by surprise and began working on the collie, and I felt hope rise.

"Mine's good; move it to the SUV," Klutz said, and Gauntlet bent and picked up the poor pit bull. Sirens and lights flashed in the distance, and I guessed the cops were arriving. Focused, I ignored the commotion around me as Klutz and I struggled to save the last two dogs. As soon as I declared them stable, Nando organised a uniformed escort back to my clinic. On arrival, Winnie was already waiting, and the three operating rooms were set up and ready to go.

Bless Winnie, that would save us time cleaning the room in between surgeries. It also allowed me to move from theatre to theatre while Winnie cleaned the one I exited. Great thinking on her behalf. Klutz watched the other sedated dogs as I rushed the Border Collie into the room. As I scrubbed, I prayed I had the skills to save those innocent animals.

Ten hours later, I stretched tiredly and rolled my shoulders. To my shock and horror, we'd lost one of the Dobermans but saved the other four. The long operating hours had been punctured between operations, with Calamity forcing food down my throat. Even if it was just a sandwich. The reception area had remained full of the uncut brothers and Drake. Nando had joined after a while. Justin Goldberg, Nando's partner, was still on the scene. The fact the barn hadn't burned meant it was a valuable cache of clues. Forensics were crawling over the place.

Wearily, I walked out of the operating theatre and straight into Calamity's arms. I was beyond exhausted but knew we'd saved four precious lives. Calamity sat me down on a bench as I curled up into his chest.

Klutz was giving Nando an update and statement at the same time. He'd aided as a nurse while Winnie scrubbed the rooms clean. I was thankful this kind and caring man had taken up animal medicine. Because as wonderful as a human doctor he'd have been, he was hands down better with animals. Tired, I closed my eyes and let the hum of conversation drift over me. I was shattered and needed to sleep a good eight hours.

But I'd be lucky to get four. With no other vet present, it would be down to me to keep a check on the dogs through the next twenty-four hours. My eyes fell shut, and I snuggled into Calamity.

When I awoke, I was horrified to see bright sunlight and knew it was well past midday. I flew out of bed and rushed downstairs to find Calamity, Blaze, and Jon staring at me in surprise.

"Who turned off my alarm?" I cried.

"Me," Calamity answered.

"No!" I wailed. "Calam, I have to check the animals!"

"Rosie, I called a friend in. He sat with them the whole time. All four are doing well and responding to treatment," Jon replied calmly as I gazed around wild-eyed. I'd slept over twelve hours, judging by the clock.

"What friend?" I demanded, and Jon chuckled.

"My cousin. Kenny was heading this way for the centre's opening and agreed to step in for a few days and give you a hand."

"He's qualified?"

"Rosie," Jon chided with a roll of his eyes. Okay, that told me. Still tired, I sank into a chair and made grabby hands at Calamity. He rose to his feet and made me a drink.

"Thought pregnant women couldn't have caffeine?" Blaze asked, confused.

"Oh no, Rosie has substituted hot chocolate for coffee. Now she's a fiend if her hot chocolate isn't ready." Calamity chuckled, and I glowered. Huh, I'll give him fiend. I was baking his baby here.

"Don't upset the pregnant one," I mumbled and grabbed the mug from Calamity. He'd put my marshmallows and whipped cream on top. Happily, I sent him a blinding smile and cradled the cup carefully.

"Never," Blaze said. "I'm here to let you know

somebody is gonna provide security on the clinic for the next few weeks until we catch and shut these assholes down, Rosie. We'll also have someone at the rescue centre in case they target it looking for dogs. Jon's moved his rescues here now, and we must be careful."

"Not a problem. Call Hawthorne's and Juno Group to see if they could increase security and personnel. Money isn't an issue," I said after glancing at Calamity to check.

He merely nodded in agreement.

"Yeah, I can do that," Blaze agreed.

"How is everyone?"

"Bummed we never caught them, but we were so damn close. There were ten dead dogs in that barn. Nando thinks they've stopped dropping them at dump sights and just plan to burn the venue. Much easier, with no cleanup or anything. That's going to be a fucker if the assholes use that strategy," Blaze snarled.

"There must be a way to track them," I mused.

"Jacob, he can call on… shall we say higher help?" Calamity asked, and I turned to him.

"Think he'd do that for a dog fighting ring?"

"Yeah. Dog fighting is a massive crime and often funds other crimes. I'll phone Casey and ask her to request Jacob's support." Calamity nodded. If we accessed Jacob's aid, I knew we'd find those assholes much quicker.

"Can't see Jacob saying no," Blaze agreed.

Jon looked confused but said nothing.

"Then we'll put in a call. Jon, do you need anything for your opening next week?" Calamity asked.

"No, everything is set up. The rescue centre is as perfect as possible. The architect drew up my ideal plan, and the builder constructed it. Kenny is planning on hanging around for a while. He recently quit his job in California and came here to lick his wounds. Won't go into details but woman trouble."

"Is Kenny looking for a job?" I asked, perking up. Calamity laughed.

"Maybe I've not spoken to him yet, apart from the emergency last night. Kenny's a good guy. He might settle down here. Wouldn't mind having some family close," Jon mused.

"If he can get me his resume, I'll take a look," I offered. I'd been searching for a new vet but had not found someone I could get along with. In fact, after several disastrous interviews, I pulled the ad for a while.

"You got a vacancy?" Jon asked, looking confused.

"I have all staff apart from one extra vet. The third space I'm keeping for Klutz. I'd also like an emergency on-call vet for out-of-hours. But if Kenny and I get along, maybe we can find a fourth to fit with the rest of us," I suggested.

Jon sat back, and a frown crossed his face.

"I may know someone. Jan works great with a small team but prefers on-call and out-of-hours. His present job is forcing him to do day shifts, and he is really unhappy. And he's got a great skill set, from everyday pets to the exotic. Jan also worked in a zoo

217

for a couple of years. His name's Jan Pixey. I can get Jan to phone you?" Jon offered.

I swapped glances with Calamity, who nodded.

"Sure. That would be wonderful," I said warmly.

If I hired them, I knew Calamity would have a deep dive done on them. In fact, as I considered the hirings, Calamity was already getting their surnames and locations from Jon. He blithely gave Calamity the information needed to have Hawthorne's run their checks. Blaze met my eyes over our mugs, and we grinned.

Our opening day at the clinic went swimmingly. Kenny and I got on so well he'd been hired within hours. Many locals signed up, and many of my old customers followed me to the new clinic. Word had got out of our rescuing the poor dogs and loads of people dropped donations in to pay for their care, which was so sweet. Penny's food had been snatched as quickly as it came out, to our amusement, and everyone had a great time.

There were many inquiries about the rescue centre that Jon was opening, and he spent a lot of time explaining how canines used in fighting could be rehabilitated. Jon had several brochures showing his successes, and the vibe around the clinic was good. Winnie had designed a questionnaire asking how the community felt about an animal sanctuary. She also asked about the possibility or a rehousing centre not just for dogs but all abandoned animals. Both suggestions were met with positive reactions.

Many people were tired of seeing healthy animals euthanised because of budget cuts. I didn't have a problem with budgets. I had my own personal one, who was determined to see I got what I needed. Someone even suggested that unwanted animals could be dropped off at any vet clinic, and we would pick them up for free. It was a good idea and one I took on board. It should save some poor animals from being dumped at the roadside. I considered asking the RCPD and RCFD if they would also be open to taking in pets that no one wanted, and we would collect them the same day.

Everything was going wonderfully, except one thing nagged at me. Calamity and his aversion to drawing. I could see how it tortured him. He was so creative, and it had to be killing him not to draw. After that attempt where he had screwed it up and thrown a tantrum, I'd not seen him pick up a pencil. It was almost as if he'd given up on ever drawing and creating his beautiful works of art again. The children's home was becoming more of a possibility. Calamity mentioned it more, seeming to settle his hopes on helping children like him.

While it was a wonderful idea, it wasn't Calamity. He was wild and free, and he somehow needed to be reminded of that. Hell, he'd not even touched his Harley yet. It sat in my garage, gathering dust, and I knew Hayleigh had given him permission to ride. But Calamity avoided it as much as he did his art book. Clyde would not break my man, and while I accepted

Calamity was fractured, he was healing. Quiet discussions with Klutz told me that the mental damage to Calamity would take longer to heal. Clyde had stolen everything that Calamity had held dear, his safety, security, and right to live as he believed.

Klutz explained the therapist was helping Calamity along, and I had seen improvements. I accepted Calamity may never be exactly the same as the man I fell in love with. But as therapy helped, I saw more of the old Calamity resurface. I wished he'd regain his confidence, ride his Harley, and draw again. Because I had every faith in him, yet I didn't know how to help him restore the faith in himself. There had to be a way. I just needed to discover how.

Chapter Twelve.

Calamity

I was shocked at my next therapy session to see an art book and pencils in front of where I usually sat. My gaze narrowed on the pad, and my mind instantly turned away. Dan, my therapist, watched with sharp eyes and noted my aversion.

"That triggered something," Dan said.

"Triggered a lot of things. And I don't wanna draw," I replied.

"What do you wish to talk about?" Dan encouraged.

"Don't know. There's bad shit happening in the world today. This Covid-19 is running rampant, states and countries are shutting down, yet South Dakota isn't instituting anything. I see facemasks on the street, but they are not mandatory, and that frightens me."

"Why do they scare you?" Dan asked, picking up on that.

"Because I can't see their faces. They're hidden from me. I don't know if there's a possible attacker behind the mask, an old enemy or somebody going about their everyday routine. It's making me antsy," I admitted.

"What else do you feel?"

"Frightened that someone may attack. At home, Rosie has also instigated extra measures. People are to park in the car lot, and one nurse will come and collect their pet. And all payments are made with card machines. All the staff are tested daily for this fuckin' illness. Anyone with a temperature is sent home for three days while being monitored. Winnie and the nurses are constantly cleaning and sterilising after each client. The whole situation shits the life out of me," I said honestly.

"Covid-19 is a frightening aspect. In the States and other countries, it's running rampant. People are dying in droves, and it's terrifying to know we're living in a pandemic. The question I have, Calamity, is what can you do to change life to make you safe?"

Good question. I relaxed and chewed it over. Dan had seen straight to the heart of the issue. It wasn't so much Covid-19 I was frightened of. The problem was, what could I do to manage another situation out of my control?

"Rosie and I have limited our contact with other people. My brothers and I FaceTime a lot. Blaze needs to stay healthy because Ali-kat relies on him for the farm. Klutz has locked himself up in Rosie's house and attends online classes now. Jon and his cousin Kenny keep their distance, and we communicate with a big space between us. Everybody wears face masks, although they're not mandatory. Rosie, Klutz, and the staff at the clinic have tons of supplies of PPE. Rosie is even funding free help for pets whose owners have been fired because of Covid or had hours reduced," I finally answered.

"So if you and everyone around you are working hard to stop the spread of this disease, what is your worry?"

"Why hasn't the fuckin' state been locked down? Other states are! Hell, England, France, and Germany have closed borders, locked their countries down, and even forced everyone to work from home. They're being battered by Covid, and their governments have acted to protect as many lives as possible. Why hasn't South Dakota followed suit? Why aren't we being ordered to care for ourselves? People are dying!" I exploded, and Dan nodded.

"And that makes you angry."

"Yes, it makes me fuckin' furious. Do we mean so little to our governing bodies? The cases of positive results are rising rapidly, yet… hey… go about your everyday lives. Don't lock down, do not protect everyone by wearing a mask. Yeah, a mask doesn't stop you from catching it, but it stops you from spreading it if you have it. I don't understand!" I cried angrily.

"Can you tell me how this relates to your attack?"

My head jolted back in surprise.

"It doesn't."

"Calamity, that was a knee-jerk reaction. Compare the two situations and let me know what you discover," Dan announced calmly.

Dan's eyes watched me intently. I drew a deep breath and calmed myself before thinking about what Dan had asked me.

"Both were out of my control. And both could have possibly ended my life," I finally spoke. Dan nodded in encouragement.

"With both, I am helpless to defend myself, and I hate that. Clyde controlled my captivity; the Governor controls my safety and health. Those with Covid-19 are not staying at home but are out spreading it. We have a right to protection, whether we defend ourselves from each other or our own tendencies. Other people are making decisions which affected my life or affect me in both situations."

"Keep going, Calamity," Dan urged encouragingly.

I frowned.

"And I can't save anyone, let alone myself, in both scenarios. I couldn't stop Clyde from taking me. And I can't stop some idiot with Covid-19 passing me in the street and infecting other innocents and me."

"Because you have a hero complex, Calamity?" Dan asked, and I reared back, startled again.

"No," I drew the word out. "It's because I don't enjoy seeing anyone hurt and harmed through the actions of others. Whether it's Covid-19, Clyde, a rapist, murderer, or serial killer, their victims suffer. And I can relate to their victims because I was one when younger. And Clyde opened that scabbed-over wound. Clyde made me feel like a victim again with his behaviour. And Covid-19 makes me feel the same way. That triggers my helplessness to save people."

"You avoided the answer, Calamity. Do you have a hero complex?" Dan pushed.

Well, damn, I thought I'd just answered that.

"No, but I respect that everyone has the right to feel safe and live as they wish, as long as it doesn't harm others. That's not a hero; that is somebody with respect."

"So, have you saved people during this pandemic?" Dan asked, and I shrugged. "Calamity think. You own three major businesses. What have you done to help them?"

"I informed Scott that anyone who wishes to work from home can. They're expected to work a full day but can stay safe. If they test positive for Covid, they'll have the full backing of the companies with whatever they need. I told Scott to pay for medical care if they don't have insurance. Honestly, they should all be covered by the company policy anyway.

"If somebody has time off because someone in their household has Covid and requires care, they'll be paid. If they are voluntarily self-isolating because of health risks to themselves, then they'll be paid in full. And if there's a death, then we'll help them during their grieving."

"What else could you do, or have you done?" Dan

225

urged.

I talked about the other plans I'd put into place for faceless staff I had never met. And the support I provided for everyone employed by one of my companies.

"Can you do anything differently?" Dan inquired.

"No."

"So, in your own way, you are shielding those you could reach within your sphere of influence. You are caring for people, Calamity, even if you can't see their faces."

I rocked back at that. Because I'd not seen it that way. But Dan was correct. I was still saving individuals. And then the epiphany hit. Shit, I didn't need to be part of Rage to save innocents. I, Calamity, was doing that right now.

"Calamity, pay attention to your right hand," Dan commented after a few minutes.

I glanced down, and my jaw dropped open. The whole time during the difficult talk, I'd been sketching, and it was perfect. I'd drawn a bike tank and, inside the lines, sketched a graveyard scene with roses surrounding it. Picking the pad up, I stared at the detail of the flowers and tombstones.

"I wasn't even aware I was drawing," I murmured.

"That's beautiful. And I see nothing wrong with it at all."

"Thank you."

"For?" Dan asked.

"For distracting me from my fear that I'd never be skilled to draw these works of art again. And allowing me the space to explore," I said honestly.

Dan grinned.

"That's my job. And now you know you can. I expect to see more artwork at our next appointment. And Calamity, you're not alone in your fears. Today we wore masks, but I'm offering FaceTime sessions to all my clients. And so far, ninety per cent have taken them. Please schedule your appointment, in person or online, with Melanie as you leave."

I grinned at Dan, knowing that I wasn't alone. Despite our governor's lack of action and the high rate of positive results terrifying us daily, people were taking responsibility.

Rosie

I watched as Calamity stepped into the garage. Something had happened in therapy. He'd returned with a new awareness in his eyes. Calamity was relaxed, open, and smiling, unlike his usual sessions, where he returned thoughtful and contemplative. I stiffened as Harley pipes roared, and I ran through the house to stand on the porch as Calamity walked the bike out.

"Want a ride?" he asked with a cheeky smile.

I hurried inside to collect my riding jacket and helmet. We wouldn't go far because I was pregnant. But even to the bottom of the drive was something.

Calamity

The feeling of suffocation finally left me as Rosie gripped me from behind, and we took a steady ride. I wasn't ashamed of going slower than I usually would because I had precious cargo on board. Rosie and I headed into the hills, and I knew exactly where I was heading. When I pulled up outside Magic's, I saw a few bikes, but none belonging to Rage. Rosie and I donned face masks, and Rosie had a couple of pairs of gloves for us to put on.

On opening the door, I noticed Magic's wasn't as crowded as usual, and to my surprise, only one club was present. Lance from the Fallen Warriors rose to his feet.

"Magic's is closed to anyone apart from the Fallen Warriors," Lance called out.

I frowned in surprise.

"Sorry, Lance, we didn't know," I said, and Lance twisted his head from where he'd been sitting back down.

Magic shot up and stared from behind the bar.

"Calamity?" Lance urged, surprised.

"Yeah, sorry, we'll leave," I replied.

"Sit your ass down, son! Fuckin' missed your smiling face," Magic boomed.

He pointed to the end of the bar, and Rosie and I made our way to it.

"What's going on?" I asked.

"With this covid crap, I've locked the bar to those who ain't my regular MCs. And I've given them all a time slot they can arrive at. Tonight is Fallen Warriors, and Hellfire has Sunday afternoon, while Unwanted Bastards have Sunday evening, for example. We shut between openings and sterilise shit, and we're keeping people healthy," Magic said, sliding a bottle of beer in my direction and a soft drink for Rosie.

"Hear congrats are in order," Lance called from where he sat with his MC.

"Yeah, Rosie's just over three months!" I replied happily.

"Glad to hear and overjoyed at seeing you on your feet, Calamity. Everyone was fuckin' worried about you when the news hit. Telling ya our prayers were with you, kid," Lance said warmly.

I nodded, happy to be accepted by the Fallen Warriors and not chased out for being a nomad now.

"And you, little lady, you've been busy," Magic stated, and Rosie lit up and began revealing what we'd been up to.

We spent three hours with everyone, explaining everything and catching up on the news. Lance was intrigued by my plan to help kids like me, who would be written off in the foster system. He said that if I got it up and running to let him know, he and his guys could work on their fitness and give them apprenticeships. That hit home hard. Despite being an outcast from Rage, I still had a support network. The ride back was easy, and as filled with happiness as I was.

Rosie

I picked up the phone with a yawn. The ringing had woken me up out of a deep sleep. I wasn't on call tonight, so I did not know who was calling.

"Rosie, we have found the dog ring. Could you get anyone and everyone who's trained? RCPD is ready to move and close this place down, but we can hear dogs screaming and know we've got some injured canines," Drake said. His voice was pissed, and anger simmered below the surface.

"Send me an address. I'll bring help," I replied. I hung up as Calamity opened his eyes and sat up.

"Rage found the dog ring. They need support with injured animals," I announced.

Calamity jumped out of bed as I called Kenny, Klutz, and Jon.

We all brought SUVs, knowing we'd have to carry injured animals. Jan hadn't arrived yet, the night on-call vet, although he was due any day now. Calamity led the way on his Harley as we followed him one by one out to a barn near Alison's farm. As I climbed out, I noticed a crowd on their knees with guys surrounding them. From what I could see, RCPD was in force alongside Rage and several other MCs. Hawthorne's and the Juno Group were also present.

And to my surprise, Jacob's men were milling around in dark combats.

"What do you have?" I asked as Nando approached.

"Got a trailer where the unfought dogs are. Seems owners brought them in and placed them inside. Easy storage and easy to escape should they be raided. They weren't expecting Delta Force to land on them. We have multiple arrests and injured animals. Some ain't letting anyone get near. They are aggressive and snapping at rescue attempts," Nando said.

"Jon, sedate those that are aggressive, and then can you load and move them to the rescue centre if they're unharmed? Klutz, start basic first aid and sedate dogs if they are snappy. Do not risk fingers or hands in treating them. Kenny, access each dog and use the black, red, and yellow markers. Those with black we'll euthanise immediately on my second assessment. No point in letting them suffer," I said with a choking noise. Tears were lodged in my throat, but I had a job right now, and those poor animals needed me.

I scowled at the prisoners as we marched past them and into the barn. The smell of blood rose and threatened to make me vomit. Jon disappeared into the trailer with a tranquilliser gun while Klutz was already wrapping bandages around a Pit Bull Terrier. Kenny was on his knees, accessing the bodies of eight dogs. We'd been too late to stop their fights, but at least the rest were uninjured. Five minutes later, I'd agreed with Kenny's assessments, and we had to put two canines down.

"This is murder," I whispered as I worked frantically over the body of a Doberman bitch. Her eyes were open, and almost begging me to let her go. She'd been given a sedative to keep her calm while I wrapped her wounds and performed emergency surgery on the ground. It would hold until I got her back to the clinic.

"Jon is taking the trailer with Blaze, Gauntlet, and Wild. They're going to move the dogs into cages Jon has for them," Ace spoke from behind.

"Okay. This pretty lady is stable. Put her in the cage in my backseat," I said to Ace and moved on to the next. It took Kenny and me twenty minutes to stabilise him while Klutz worked on the minor wounds. Cars were leaving as we handed each dog over, and they were rushed to the clinic. Finally, I climbed into my car, knowing we'd only lost two dogs so far, and I followed a trail of headlights to my home.

On arrival at the clinic, I discovered Winnie organising everyone while people milled around. All three surgeries and examination rooms were open. I was surprised to see a tall, dark-skinned man accessing each dog as they came in and directing the human carrying it where to place it.

"Who the hell are you?" I demanded, approaching quickly.

"Jan, pretty lady. Now, are you Rosie?" he asked.

"Yes, this is my clinic," I responded, and he nodded.

"Right, this is the situation," Jan said and began telling me the worst wounded were already in theatre.

Kenny was in with the female Doberman, working to stabilise her. Jan had a Pit Bull in the second theatre, and I had a Bulldog.

"If you are coming in with a victim, mask up and sterilise your hands," Winnie bellowed from the entrance. "If you're waiting on news, please wait outside and keep your distance from everyone!"

The two other nurses dashed past me to support Jan and Kenny while Calamity took over from Winnie, bellowing orders and freeing her to help me. We toiled long into the night and morning. Kenny was with one Dogo Argentino for six hours, carefully stitching a wound to its heart. A canine had clearly burrowed into his body with powerful jaws. It made me sick to think of the dogs fighting like this while owners and punters cheered them on.

One female Rottweiler nearly had her throat torn out, and it took all my skill to stop her from bleeding out. At one point, Nando ordered uniformed officers to other vets to get blood and fluids as we began running out. Two vets arrived on hearing our plight and waded in, bringing the much-needed supplies and extra hands.

Jon had returned with five more wounded animals whose wounds hadn't healed from their last fight. It was sickening to think their owners would have forced them into the ring again for the sake of money. People came and went. Nando handed over to Bobby Lucas and left to interview those he'd captured. Bobby reassured us that all the detectives were interviewing those arrested, and over three hundred people had been carted to the police station.

Bobby said the station was so overfilled they'd opened up the old jail cells hidden under the building. And when those filled, they opened the cells used two hundred years ago in the mayor's office. Several influential businessmen had been swept up in the raid, and unluckily for them, Delta Force had got wind of the fight and set up cameras covering every angle. They would be charged and unable to wriggle out of it.

At about seven in the morning, Calamity and Bobby made all the clinic staff take a half-hour break and eat and drink. We were all tired, but we still needed to care for some wounded animals. I saw Drake and Calamity talking intensely, and Calamity was putting his point across firmly. Drake was nodding at whatever Calamity was saying while Blaze and Ace listened intently. Blaze said something, and then Ace did, and all four men began closing together to have a deeper conversation.

I didn't know or care what they were arguing over. I required food and drink and then returned to work. Finally, I sat down at eleven in my office with a groan, and within minutes, I'd laid my head on my arms and closed my eyes. Sleep hit hard, and I drifted away. I was so tired I never felt arms pick me up and carry me off.

I awoke in our bed, and much like the last time I'd worked through the night, I leapt out and raced downstairs. It was dark outside, and I guessed I'd slept the day away. Calamity, Klutz, Kenny, and Jon were in the kitchen drinking coffee, and I sniffed and turned green at the thought of caffeine. Calamity handed me a hot chocolate, and I sank gratefully into a chair.

"The dogs survived the night. Two are in terrible shape but fighting to live. As long as they fight for the next twenty-four hours, they'll survive," Kenny said.

"Who is at the clinic?"

"Local vets have been covering it all day, and Jan is on call for tonight. There'll be another vet present in case he's needed as he's on standby for an emergency. Old Lady Hudson has a cow that seems to be having a slow birth. Jan is aware he might have to answer her call," Kenny said with a yawn.

"We've ordered food, chicken and fries okay?" Calamity asked me as my stomach growled.

"It better arrive soon, or the fridge won't be safe. I'll eat everything in that fucker," I quipped, and Calamity laughed.

"Is Jan okay to cover tonight?" I urged.

"Yeah, Jan wants night work and to sleep during the day. We'll be back on our normal rotation tomorrow," Klutz said, and I nodded.

"The clinic was sterilised?" I sought worried about this fuckin' pandemic.

"Yes, and the relieving vets tested negative for Covid and brought their own nurses to clean. We've not had a single positive case yet, Rosie, which I think is thanks to our stringent cleaning," Calamity answered. There was a knock at the door, and Cowboy walked in, bringing buckets of delicious-smelling food.

"Oh, thank God!" I exclaimed and pounced on him.

Cowboy stepped back as I yanked a bucket from him, dumped it on the table, and dived in. Calamity laughed as he waved Cowboy to sit and join us while I tore the chicken from the bone.

"Here's a plate, baby," Calamity said, putting one on the table. He placed two chicken breasts, fries, onion rings and nuggets in front of me, and I pulled a third piece from the bucket.

"Holy fuck," Cowboy finally exclaimed.

"Don't get between a pregnant woman and her food," Calamity advised.

"No shit," Cowboy replied as I sank my teeth into a drumstick I snatched from Kenny's plate. Kenny didn't say a word and just merely replaced it. I was starving, and the baby was too. I was not apologising for anything. As we ate, they gave me updates on the injured dogs and which were most at risk over the next twenty-four hours.

I was warmed by the dedication shown by other vets who'd arrived to help and made mental notes to send thank you hampers to them. It was great how the local community had banded together to support these poor animals.

"Nando is dropping a supply of dog food off at the rescue. RCPD had a whip round to collect money for the dog's rehab. Although they decided the food would be more helpful. But the Juno Group, Hawthorne's and Delta Force have made a cash donation to be split between the clinic and the centre. Rage is also sending a truck full of food," Calamity mentioned, and I nodded.

"That what you were discussing with Drake?" I asked carefully.

"No, baby. I can't discuss that conversation, but shit's progressing," Calamity said.

Progressing? What the hell did that mean? I know he'd been trying to get Blaze and the others to return to Rage. Drake clearly hadn't accepted their resignations, as he would lose half the damn club. So what was Calamity up to?

Chapter Thirteen.

Calamity

This would make or break Rage. I knew it. Drake and Texas knew it, and so did everyone else present. Drake had contacted old ladies, princesses, and uncut brothers and asked them to attend a meeting that I had proposed. Klutz was stuck to Rosie's side like a limpet, and I appreciated his loyalty. Although I hoped at the end of this shit, it would all be unnecessary anymore. Because he was Hellfire, Micah couldn't be present but I knew he was at the end of the phone should I need to get Rosie out of here.

"Calamity requested us to call a meeting, so I'm going to hand it over to him," Drake said loud enough to cut through the dull murmur of conversation.

I took a deep breath and stepped up.

"Drake, Texas, and this lot fucked up. They know it, and so do we. For three months, we've punished them and made it clear we won't put up with their behaviour anymore. I think they get the point. Drake is moving Rage forward, but he is torn between loyalty to his dad and the rules the founders set up and devotion to those coming in new. So I'm asking everyone to listen to what Drake says and at least acknowledge he's meeting us all halfway."

I sat back next to Rosie and let Drake lead.

This was in his hands.

Drake

"As Calamity pointed out, we fucked up big time. In the past, princesses were off limits, but for a reason we forgot. In Bulldog's generation, a princess could be bargained with to claim status and money. Those days are gone, but we're still fighting them in our minds. Old ladies don't get a vote in Rage policies. This is a man's riding club. But we disrespected them with the old rules of allowing whores. Forgetting we are no longer the MC that Bulldog runs once again. So today, I want to go through Rage's charter, one rule at a time, and I demand every brother's agreement on whether the law stays or goes.

"Ladies, while you are welcome to voice an opinion, you don't get a vote. But today and today alone, you can speak freely without worrying you're shaming your old man or fear of repercussions. We require your opinions and thoughts," I said and swallowed hard.

"Why now, Drake?" Jett demanded. Oh, that clever little prick. As much as I loved that kid, I hated him sometimes.

"Because we're renewing Rage. New clubhouse, ground design, different garage layout, etc. But we forgot to look at the charter and the behaviours that drive the charter we swear allegiance to. And sometimes, we need a sledgehammer over our heads, Jett, to remind us of shit. We screw up, and then we fix it, as you know," I said.

Jett's eyes narrowed. He knew I was referring to the number of times he'd screwed up with Sin and wouldn't take advice.

"Fair point. What do we get out of it?" Lindsey demanded.

"This is your chance to help stamp out the shit that annoys the fuck out of you. Either use it or lose it," I retorted.

Lindsey's gaze tightened.

"Simple, ban skanks, barflies, whores, club bunnies, and any bitch who doesn't belong to a brother." Autumn looked at me.

"Done. That was voted weeks ago," I said easily.

"Only females visiting Rage are old ladies, friends, and those the brother's date. No more bringing one-night stands. You wanted a family club; now you fuckin' earn it," Penny spat, and I heard the anger in her voice.

"Not arguing," I soothed, and she sat back with a

suspicious glare.

"What's your end goal, Drake?" Rosie demanded.

"My MC made whole. We all do. We've spoken a lot over the weeks and realise that we sided with Texas for several reasons. One because of the old rules. No brother dated a princess, but I explained we forgot why. And two, because it's conditioned in us to stick together. Which is why we felt so fuckin' betrayed when Calamity and Klutz resigned. And why it hurts like fuck Blaze and the rest refuse to wear their cuts. Rosie, girl, we're trying to create a club we can be proud of. Just because we shove our head in the sand and say that's the way we have always done shit doesn't mean it's right," I replied.

"Not a bad answer. So why are Calamity and Klutz here?" Rosie urged.

"Because we want them to rejoin us, take their rightful cuts back, and everyone else as well. But Calamity and Klutz won't do crap until we hash this mess out. So, can we get on with it?" I asked.

"Sure, but don't get pissy if you hate what we say," Artemis drawled, eyes narrowed on me, looking for a trick.

One by one, I read through the charter rules. Many remained the same, but several were changed. And the women helped influence the new rules. The club whores were gone. Protecting the old ladies and children continued to be a priority. Rage remaining legal was paramount and a fair vote amongst brothers. We were returning to the old way of needing to nominate and second motions but leaving an appeal process open if need be. The president's final word was law, and there was no going against him.

Princesses could date full brothers, and there would be no sneaking around behind our backs. The ring remained in place, although the women disagreed. They didn't like the idea of their men being beaten for fucking up badly. But we needed that rule in place. After Jacked and Gid's betrayal, we wouldn't risk another. Other hard fast laws stayed, but once we'd rounded out the charter, only a few rules required changing.

Was it that easy?

"Yes, Drake," Phoe said softly, reading my face.

"Really?" I asked her, moving closer to where she stood.

"Yeah. Because we don't want to change the club or the men we married. We wanted to be respected and heard."

"But you were always honoured," I denied.

"Not with your past whores shoved in our faces; we weren't. Or having to watch night after night to see if we needed to stop a skank attacking our man. The old ladies could never relax fully on Rage."

"I never noticed," I muttered.

"And that was the point of the last three months. None of you realised, apart from Calamity and Klutz. Now you need to make it right with those boys," Phoe said and planted a gentle kiss on my lips.

I placed a box on the bar as I squeezed her tightly and walked toward Texas. I opened the lid and removed the first cut. I looked at the name and handed it to Texas. His large hands clenched it tightly, and he turned to face everyone.

"I acted like a motherfuckin' asshole and wouldn't admit I was wrong. I'd like you to accept your place in Rage with my nomination and support," Texas stated, looking at Calamity.

"Seconded!" Axel boomed.

A soft chuckle left my lips. Axel had been a bear with a sore head since Calamity walked out. With the chance of putting our family back together, Axel was in favour of anything that made that happen.

"I'll not give Rosie up," Calamity added into the silence.

"You got my blessing," Texas rumbled.

His gaze shot to Rosie, who stood stone-faced by Calamity. Sadly, I noted damage had been done to their relationship. Rosie would no longer turn to Texas for help, and I helped facilitate that. She'd never trust her father one hundred per cent again. That shit cut deep. Calamity exchanged a glance with Rosie, and I could see their unspoken communication. Hunter had been correct when he called them soulmates. Calamity stepped forward, his face expressionless.

"I'll accept," he said, and Texas beamed, and Calamity twisted, and Texas helped him put the cut on. Calamity ran his fingers down the front of his cut and stopped as they caught on a new patch. With a frown, Calamity studied the new patch. Embroidered on it was a single word, Conscience.

"I don't understand?" Calamity asked, puzzled.

"Because you and Klutz are the conscience of the club Calamity, and we never realised it until you both stood up to us. One a boy, barely a man, and one a prospect bordering on brother. That badge is a sign of respect from all of us present. And should you choose to share your wisdom, Rage will always be better with you," I explained.

"Thank you so... oof," Calamity broke off as Rosie hit him full length and dragged his head down for a kiss.

Calamity waved a hand, telling us to continue while we chuckled at him.

"Klutz," Ace called.

"Seconded," Axel boomed, and we laughed.

No one else was getting a word in tonight. Klutz swapped glances with Aurora Victoria, and they moved together.

"I won't give him up if he's a prospect," Aurora stated.

"Not giving her up, so I'll pass," Klutz said. Ace and Axel exchanged a look, and then Axel shoved Klutz into a headlock while Ace wrestled his cut on him. Axel released him immediately as Aurora stared at Klutz.

"Oh!" she exclaimed happily.

Klutz peered at the two new patches. Brother, the top one proclaimed, and the second matched Calamity's patch.

"Ain't you meant to vote?" Klutz growled as he rearranged his tee.

"We did. And it took a real brother to force us to

realise what we needed. And that's the type of man we want here, building our future. You keep your head down, are quiet, and get overlooked. But you have the same qualities Calamity has, Klutz, and we missed that. Not anymore," I said.

No, I'd not fuck up leading this group of amazing men and women again. President was my legacy, but I believed I made the role. I didn't. The role shaped me.

One by one, brothers stepped up, holding cuts for those that had taken them off in protest. And one by one, they were slipped back over shoulders and sighs echoed through the room.

Rosie

"Are you happy?" I asked Calamity.

He kept stroking his cut, and the shock on his face was genuine. Calamity honestly thought he wouldn't get into Rage.

"Over the moon, I've got everything to live for."

"Love you, Calam," I whispered.

"Don't know what I did to deserve you, but I love you both as much," I said, cradling her belly.

"You are a good man. One that was harmed, and I don't warrant forgiveness for my part. But I am gonna work at being the best father-in-law you could wish for, Calamity. I don't deserve the chance, but I'm going to bust my balls for my place in your lives," Dad's voice came over Calamity's shoulder.

I turned in Calamity's arms and studied Dad's face. Tonight, by swallowing his pride, he'd earned that title back. The road to forgiveness would be long, and there'd be stumbles along the way, but I didn't doubt Dad's sincerity right now.

"Thank you," Calamity responded.

"Swear to you both. I'll make it up to you. And the baby," Texas said with awe.

I smiled at Dad.

"This was a surprise but not unwanted. Nor unloved. And you're welcome to mend bridges, but I will always pick Calamity. He deserves nothing less," I announced strongly.

"No, he doesn't. And I know I'm going to be fuckin' proud to introduce him as my son-in-law. Now, when's the wedding?" Texas asked, and I rolled my eyes.

"In two weeks, Axel's handling it, and the old ladies are ready to jump in with the planning," Calamity replied with a cheeky grin. "Say yes to marrying me, Rosie, mine."

"Yes!" I squealed as Calamity slid a diamond ring on my finger. I stared down at the twinkle before looking up and throwing myself into his arms.

"We're going to have a beautiful life," Calamity promised me, and I didn't doubt him.

Epilogue.

Drake

"You understand we'll never be completely clean?" I said to Calamity as he stood outside and watched the sky. Inside, everyone was celebrating Calamity's engagement to Rosie.

"Yeah, I know, Drake. And I'll be a part of the grey area, ensuring Rage protects what we have," Calamity replied.

"Maybe your children will inherit a club that doesn't need the grey?" I suggested.

Calamity shook his head.

"No, because Rage will stand forever against those who wish to harm innocents. That's the type of club Rage has become, and it won't change."

"Shit, Calamity, I look at you and see myself before Da died. Full of hope and plans, and I'm wondering where I fucked up," I said honestly.

"It went wrong, Drake, because scum infiltrated Rage and tried to steal a legacy that wasn't theirs. That boy remains in your heart somewhere, brother. You need to release him to play sometimes. Don't let the rest of your life be lived in the darkness. You have light now, Drake; cling to that," Calamity said.

"You were a punk kid when Rage took you in. Got no idea how wise you'd become over the years. But I'm fuckin' proud of the man you grew into," I replied.

Calamity nodded.

"Only became that guy because of my brothers and a man I call friend," Calamity murmured and reached for my shoulder. Calamity gripped me tightly, and I noticed the loss of strength in his grip.

"Leave you with your thoughts, Drake, but don't think about what ifs and maybes. Consider what you have now and celebrate it like I do. I have been through hell and back these last three months, but I wouldn't alter anything because life showed me things I didn't know about myself. And I've learned and grown. And I don't honestly believe we ever will stop developing. That's human nature to roll with the blows and change with the winds," Calamity said and walked away.

"That kid will be a damn fine president one day," Texas declared, coming out of the darkness.

"Calamity needs his own chapter because where he walks, others will follow."

"Ain't disagreeing, brother. Fuck, we can be blind assholes sometimes. But that kid's self-worth and belief, he earned that. Klutz would make a great VP," I mused.

Texas laughed.

"Thought we were staying to RC," Texas said, chuckling.

"Who the fuck knows what the future holds?" I taunted and slapped Texas on the shoulder. Texas turned to me with raised eyebrows.

"I certainly didn't see a grandbaby this early!" he teased, and I roared with laughter. Somehow I knew struggles remained for Rage. But I also understood we'd make it through them because of kids like Calamity and Klutz.

Calamity

I sat in the sunlight, surrounded by the animals who were playing, holding Mrs Travis's letter in my hands. I needed to open it, but before I did, I was counting my blessings. My fingers had healed to ninety per cent, and I had sufficient dexterity to create art. My left hand, the palm, was a tight ball of muscles and nerves and would never improve over seventy per cent. As I was right-handed, my drawing was fine. The injured shoulder was stiff, and I'd never have full rotation again, but I was mobile enough to work on designs.

The brands were faded and nearly patched over. A faint outline remained, but Rosie and I had picked a tattoo to cover them, so I'd never have to suffer them again. My back had healed, and there was minor disfigurement. Wraith from Hellfire had checked my skin and said he could recreate the Rage patch easily. And also came up with a kickass full back tattoo when I was ready. Rosie wouldn't have to see the reminders of my torture again.

I'd had a knee replacement while unconscious, which felt strange, but my left kneecap had been so badly damaged I'd never have walked. But I could ride without pain. My hip offered twinges every so often, and that was something I'd accepted. As I grew older, I knew a kickass trike would be in my future, but not for the next thirty years, I hoped. My feet had healed, although sometimes they ached from where I stood around too much. Rosie and I were looking at custom-made boots to protect the nerves. And yes, I had a distinctive limp but that was not going to stop me living life.

And finally, I had a couple of scars on my face, but my hair had grown long enough to hide the indent where the bullet had pierced my skull. How I survived a shot to the head was a miracle I didn't question. The legacy of that was some memory issues and communication problems. Sometimes I knew what I wanted to say, but the words fled. And I also suffered headaches which hadn't been a problem before. But painkillers dealt with them. Somehow, I'd walked away mainly intact. Hayleigh would continue working on my muscles and health for a while longer. But I was grateful to sit here and breathe.

I looked down at the letter, and finally, I opened it

and began to read.

"Billy,

In reading this, you're aware I am dead. Do not grieve my lovely boy because I am finally with my family. The only regret I have is leaving you behind. Billy, I hate not knowing if you found a new family or discovered love. But I shall always watch over you.

Dierdre and Clyde never deserved the precious gift you were. I was the one who called child services several times because I witnessed the abuse. In the end, I took matters into my own hands and raised you myself. I know you are eighteen because each year I refresh this letter. Billy, you gave me eight remarkable years. And greedily, I wish I could have had more.

Live, Billy, seek love and friendship and banish doubt from your mind. You're a wonderful young man, and it was my privilege to have you in my life. Know that no matter what happens, you have family here waiting for you when you die. My husband, son, and I are waiting to welcome you home.

You were never a surrogate for William. You two boys were so far apart in personality, there may as well have been an ocean between you. But you became my son in my heart. You're special, Billy, never forget that. So very extraordinary. You made the darkness fade and brought light into my life again. Take the money and companies and do as you wish with them.

Maybe leave the companies to your children because you're not really interested in business like I wasn't. Open your heart, my boy, fly, let loose, and be free. Because no matter what may happen, you are adored. And I take each memory of you as treasure. Billy, any time spent with you is worth more than any precious gem.

I never told you in life, Billy, because you were a suspicious child, but I loved you with everything I could. You were my son. And I know you cherished me even though you never said the words. Live, Billy, I urge you to live.

All my love,

Your mother."

I lay back in the grass and stared at the blue sky above me. A smile crossed my lips even while tears burned my eyes.

"I love you too, Mom," I whispered, and a gentle breeze blew across my face.

Characters.

Rage MC

Drake Michaelson. DOB. 1975. Drake is third generation Rage; he was in the third lot of brothers recruited into Rage. His father started Rage MC and died before Drake was old enough to become president. Drake became VP and, in a hostile takeover, became President. Phoenix thinks he looks like Tim McGraw with longer hair. Drake has a leanness to him but has well-defined muscles and broad shoulders. Drake sports dark brown eyes with laughter lines. He's six foot four. He adopted Phoe's 16 children, and they have two of their own.

Apache. DOB 1969. Apache is a second-gen Rage; he was in the second lot of brothers recruited into Rage. He is one of Drake's enforcers. Apache has bright green eyes and is six foot two. He is of Native American origin. Apache's described as absolutely stunning, with high cheekbones and raven black hair that hangs past his shoulders. Apache's real name is Tyee (meaning Chief) Blackelk. He looks like Lou Diamond Philips. Apache is partnered with Rock in a construction company. He is married to Silvie and has two children with her.

Ace. DOB 1983. Ace is third generation Rage; he was in the third lot of brothers recruited into Rage. Ace is Drake's VP. He's described as looking like a young Lou Diamond Philips. Like his father, he is Native American. Ace has bright green eyes and is six foot two. He is described much the same as his father, absolutely stunning with high cheekbones and raven black hair that hangs past his shoulders. Ace is no stranger to violence and will do whatever it takes to protect his club. He is now married to Artemis and has several children with her.

Fish. DOB 1978. Fish's birth name is Justin Greenway. Fish is third generation Rage; he was in the third lot of brothers recruited into Rage. Fish is Drake's sergeant at arms. He's been married to Marsha for many years and have three children. Fish runs the Rage garage. Fish has a bushy beard and untamed hair, which he keeps in check with a bandana. He is tall and broadly built and has an innate kindness.

Texas. DOB 1965. Texas is a second-gen Rage; he was in the second lot of brothers recruited into Rage. Texas's full name is Blake Craven. Texas is an older man and is the MC's secretary and treasurer. He works on bike design and specialises in paintwork. He has a robust moral code but is mindful of what the MC is capable of. He once alludes to cleaning up after their messes. Texas is tall and broad, with a goatee, dark salt and pepper hair slightly too long and piercing brown eyes. He can also play the keyboard. Texas stands at six foot four, and his old lady is

Penny.

Axel. DOB 1951. Axel was one of the founders of the club, which makes him first generation Rage. He is the Chaplin of the MC. The Chaplin's role is to look after Rage's needs spiritually. Axel ensures they have their heads straight and performs their marriages and death ceremonies. He has blue eyes, a salt-and-pepper beard, and is very loud. He's built like a mountain. Axel has wild hair which hangs to his shoulders. Axel is six foot six. Axel claims an old lady, a schoolteacher called Ellen and dotes on her.

Gunner. DOB 1976. Gunner is third generation Rage; he was in the third lot of brothers recruited into Rage. Gunner is one of Drake's Enforcers at the MC. Gunner is described as having silver-grey eyes with thick lashes. His name is Cole Washington. James Washington is Gunner's brother, and they are estranged. Gunner's described as having long sandy brown hair, high cheekbones and firm, soft lips. Gunner owns four houses, three of which he rents out; he also works at Made by Rage carving wood with Manny. He pays fifty per cent with Manny into the pot. His old lady is Autumn.

Slick. DOB 1978. Slick is third generation Rage; he was in the third lot of brothers recruited into Rage. Slick loves books and is happy reading quietly. He has soft brown eyes and is heavily muscled. Slick runs a leasing company; he has over twenty properties he rents and pays fifty per cent into the pot. He also plays chess.

Manny. DOB 1983. Manny is third generation Rage;

he was in the third lot of brothers recruited into Rage. He's described as tall, sexy as in the cute boy next door way, with tousled blond hair and light amber-coloured eyes. He was beaten by Bulldog for failing to report a pregnant prostitute and then shot in the back by Bulldog's men. Manny is six foot four. He carves wood and works his own section of Made by Rage. He pays fifty per cent with Gunner into the pot. Manny enjoys playing chess.

Lowrider. DOB 1984. Lowrider is third generation Rage; he was in the third lot of brothers recruited into Rage. He has ebony hair shaved short at the sides and longer on top. He has a roman nose, full lips, and blue eyes. Lowrider has a tattoo of black flames that crawls up his throat. He's six foot three of lean, powerful muscle and tanned. (He looks like Colin Farrell.) Lowrider's actual name is Nathan Miller. Lowrider is a mechanic and makes builds from scratch. His old lady is Lindsey.

Ezra. DOB 1979. Ezra is third generation Rage; he was in the third lot of brothers recruited into Rage. He has a younger sister called Lindsey, who seeks him out. He has brown eyes, is tall and has shaggy dark hair. Ezra's a broad-shouldered man with a deep, broad chest, beautiful bone structure and a neatly trimmed goatee. (Looks like Robert Downey Junior.) Ezra owns a landscaping company which is in high demand.

Mac. DOB 1970. Mac is third generation Rage; he was in the third lot of brothers recruited into Rage. Mac's adept at playing the drums. He was shot protecting Lindsey from her ex-husband. Mac is responsible for running the bar. He is married to Casey.

Rock. DOB 1985. Rock is third generation Rage; he was in the third lot of brothers recruited into Rage. Rock is six foot four and huge. He has a goatee and a Dodge Charger he's very protective of. He runs the Blackrock construction company with Apache. Rock has soft brown eyes and dark brown hair. He is closest to Lex out of the MC. Rock and Carly adopt three orphans he and Drake saved in the floods.

Lex. DOB 1984. Lex is third generation Rage; he was in the third lot of brothers recruited into Rage. He runs the Rage shop. Lex has hazel eyes framed by thick dark lashes. He has a dimple on his right cheek.

Blaze. DOB 1992. Blaze is a fourth-generation Rage; he was in the fourth lot of brothers recruited into Rage. He became a brother in 2016. Blaze ran the parts store but stopped when he opened a gym with Hunter. He's got green eyes. Blaze is close to Carly and thinks of her as a little sister. Blaze owns a Harley Dyna Glide and a Military Enfield he restored.

Slate. DOB 1992. Slate is a fourth-generation Rage; he was in the fourth lot of brothers recruited into Rage. Became a brother in 2016. Slate runs into Penny's burning house in Rage's Heat to save her and the children with Texas. He works with Ezra in a landscaping company.

Hunter. DOB 1991. Hunter is a fourth-generation Rage; he was in the fourth lot of brothers recruited into Rage. Became a brother in 2016. Hunter is also a designer for paintwork on bikes. Hunter opened a gym with Blaze. Hunter is ripped and covered in tattoos. His old lady is Mina

Jett. DOB. 1990. Jett is a fourth-generation Rage; he was in the fourth lot of brothers recruited into Rage. Became a brother in 2015. His name is Alexander Cutter. He's described as having black hair, dark brown eyes, high cheekbones, a square jawline and firm, soft lips. He is tall and broad, lean-hipped, long-legged and as tightly muscled. Jett is a mechanic, engine designer, and paintwork designer. His old lady is Sin.

Calamity. DOB 1996. Calamity is a fifth-generation Rage; he was in the fifth lot of brothers recruited into Rage. His name is Billy Tomkins. Calamity becomes a prospect after only being on Rage for a month. He's a talented mechanic, body designer and spray painter. He interferes and stops Frenzy from harming Silvie and takes a bullet in the shoulder for Autumn. In the Rage of Angels, we discover Calamity is taking a night class for car design.

Calamity has been in love with Rosie for years but wouldn't touch her until he became a brother. He has to face his past in this book and also has to make a decision to pick either Rage or Rosie. Calamity chooses Rosie.

Prospects.

Savage. DOB 1983. Savage is a fifth-generation Rage; he was in the fifth lot of brothers recruited into Rage. Savage is thirty-two years old and is a mechanic. Savage is Mina's alt. He shares a house with Slate.

Gauntlet. DOB 1987. Gauntlet is a fifth-generation Rage; he was in the fifth lot of brothers recruited into Rage. He works in the garage.

Klutz. DOB 1989. Klutz is a fifth-generation Rage; he was in the fifth lot of brothers recruited into Rage. Klutz is a talented bartender and often pulls scenes similar to those in the film Cocktail. He's African American. Klutz's roommate was dealing drugs in college, and Klutz got swept up in the sting. The cops beat him, and then his innocence was proven, and he was freed.

Carmine. (Phoe and Drake) DOB 1996, half African American and half white; he plays for the Cubs. Carmine joined Rage in 2019. He's from Maine and was adopted in 2010. Carmine looked after Tye, Harley, and Serenity on the streets. Phoe alludes to Carmine sacrificing himself to protect Harley and Serenity.

Tyelar. (Phoe and Drake) DOB 1996, Tye is half Mexican and half Caucasian and is from Maine. Tye joined Rage in 2019. He was adopted in 2010. In the Hunter's Rage, Tyelar is playing for the Blackhawks. Carmine had to fly out and sort his head out. Tye, like Carmine, looked after Harley and Serenity. Phoe alludes to Tye sacrificing himself to protect Harley and Serenity.

Harley. DOB 1999. Harley's from Maine and was adopted in 2010. In November 2015, two seventeen-year-olds attacked Harley from behind, cracking his skull and putting him into a coma. Harley was protecting Christian. He has soft brown eyes and ash-blonde hair. Harley woke up in Nov 2016 after the flooding of Rapid City. He joined Rage in 2019. Harley is now an apprentice Blacksmith after being told he'll never make a professional baseball player.

Cody. DOB 2000. Carmine found Cody living on the streets in Colorado; he was adopted in 2011. Bullies fear Cody because he will call them on their behaviour. Cody speaks to Phoe about joining the Trusts while he is at college. He and Christian want to run them when Phoe retires. In the meantime, he wants to manage the Rebirth Trust. Cody joined Rage in 2019.

Candidates.

Wild. DOB December 1999. He is known as Jonas Valden and approached Rage to join the club when he was fifteen. His father is a well-known tattoo artist, Rio Valden. Wild takes his younger brother and runs away.

Cowboy. Dob 2002, Cowboy is hot-headed and apt to act before thinking. Wild is three years older than him and has taken care of him for several years. Cowboy is immensely loyal to his brother. He leaps from his bike to Wild's, trusting his brother will catch him. His name is Zac Valden.

Rage Old Ladies.

Phoenix. DOB 1979. Drake's old lady. She is English and left England to escape an abusive relationship. She has six children she gave birth to and adopted eleven. Phoe is exceedingly well off and runs three National Charities. The Phoenix Trust, the Rebirth Trust and the Eternal Trust. On meeting, Drake Phoe has two more children with him. Phoe has long, blond hair and is green-eyed and five foot tall. She met Hellfire MC first and is loyal to them and a Hellfire sister. Her alternative guy is Ace.

Marsha Greenway. DOB 1978. Fish's old lady and the only old lady the club has until Phoenix meets Drake. She's known to be kind and caring. Axel is Marsha's alternative guy. Although the old ladies don't have a ranking, Marsha is Phoe's VP. Marsha has blue eyes and shoulder-length brown hair.

Silvie Stanton. DOB 1982. She's claimed by Apache. Silvie's kind and generous. The MC has a lot of respect for her. She has blond, curly hair and is close to Gunner. Silvie has soft brown eyes. She takes a job at the Made by Rage shop, working for Lindsey, first helping cut material and then as a receptionist. Finally, she becomes the shop manager. Although the old ladies don't have a ranking, Silvie is Phoe's Chaplin. Her alternative guy is Gunner.

Artemis, aka Kayleigh Mitchell. DOB 1987. She has curly red hair and green eyes. She's small, dainty and muscled. She has a heart-shaped pixie face and full lips. Kayleigh was taken in by Master Hoshi, and out of her alleged death, Artemis arose.

She was part of a group called Revenge before she left and formed the Artemis group. The Artemis Group became the Juno group when she went legal with her efforts. She has combat skills and has killed many times. Artemis's alternative guy is Drake. She is Phoe's equivalent of an enforcer. Artemis now has a large team working for her on search and rescue for child and women trafficking. She also provides protection, and James Washington makes use of her skills. She's extremely expensive.

Sinclair Montgomery. DOB 1993. Sin takes over her father's shop, the Reading Nook, when he dies, and they turn it into something special with Reid. Sin was an only child, and Reid became her surrogate brother. She is socially awkward and inept and feels out of place in crowds. She's described as dainty with brown hair and big blue eyes. Sin doesn't think she's pretty, but people describe her as beautiful. She has low self-esteem created by attending college and university when she was fifteen. Manny is Sin's alternative guy. Manny is Sin's alternative guy.

Penny Nelson. DOB 1976. Penny is a cook and server at Reading Nook. She loves cooking and baking and makes everything from scratch. She has a warm and caring attitude. Penny has two children, a son of five and a daughter of three. Penny has short dark hair cut into a bob and is a few pounds overweight with blue eyes and freckles. Penny is five foot six. Her alternative guy is Fish.

Lindsey Miller nee Smithson. DOB 1989. She is ten years younger than Ezra and is his baby sister. She has brown eyes with gold flecks and long waist-length brown hair with red highlights. Her face is a sweetheart shape, and she has plump lips and high cheekbones. Lindsey has her own business called Made by Rage, Designs by Lindsey. While Lindsey is wary of strangers, she has no worries about speaking her mind to the Rage brothers. She's kind and generous. Lindsey's books are published under the pen name of L. Smithson. Her alternative guy is Mac.

Autumn Rydell. DOB 1990. When Rage finds Autumn, she's on her knees, unable to cope and has no money. She resists the relationship with Gunner at first. Autumn starts work at the Rage Garage as their office girl. Calamity is her alternative guy, and Autumn is also an enforcer for Phoe. Autumn is a brunette with dark brown eyes and a sweet heart-shaped face. She is about five foot six and is slender but has curves in the right place.

Carly Lennon. DOB 1997. She has long dark brown hair and enormous brown eyes. Carly arrived at Made by Rage underweight and traumatised. Lindsey and Silvie decided to look after her. Rock worships the ground Carly walks on. She and Rock adopt three orphans. Blaze is her alternative.

Ellen Keating. DOB 1961. Ellen works at the Black Oak Hills Academy. Ellen has rounded curves and chestnut hair with strands of grey. Ellen usually works long hours from seven in the morning till six at night. She became the English Department Head when she was thirty-five and has held the job for twenty years.

Geneviève Angelique Blanchard. DOB 1994. Vivie is twenty-three when she meets Lex. She owns her own business, Chocolates by Geneviève. She also owns Blanchards Creations and a vineyard, amongst several other things. Vivie is a billionairess but shies away from the public. She has brown hair and green eyes and loves reading. She inherited everything from both sets of grandparents. Vivie also holds the title Duchesse Toulouse, something Lex is slightly uncomfortable with. After her attack, Vivie stopped talking, and it takes an ex-girlfriend of Lex's being mean to make her talk.

Alison Jackson. DOB 1995. Ali runs the Jackson ranch and is well thought of in the local community. When her parents died, her brother Ice Dawg moved into the farm with his biker gang. They sacked all her staff and isolated her. Ali saves Blaze from being killed by the gang and is tortured herself. Blaze protects her as he feels she suffered because of him. Ali is strong, mouthy, and not frightened to use a gun if needed. She is loyal and dedicated to raising her younger siblings. Ali's alternative is Slick.

Thomasina Mae Blake. DOB 1990. She has one sister younger than her who died, and her parents are alive, but both have divorced and remarried. Her Godfather is Walter West. Mina has been a shut-in for three years after a stalker murdered three people close to her. He stalked her for the two previous years before turning to violence. Mina was a child actress who turned into a famous actress. Since she became a shut-in, she has begun writing books about a PI under the name A. Dudley. Her alt is Savage.

Rosie Craven. (Penny and Texas) DOB 1995. Rosie is now a qualified veterinarian, and she is Texas's daughter. She's a beautiful girl with long dark hair, Slender and tall and pretty, with piercing brown eyes. She is harassed by Brett, takes a civil suit against him, and quits work. When Calamity is kicked from Rage, she stands by his side and cuts Texas and Rage off. Rosie has opened her own clinic and, with Jon, a rescue centre. She also wants to open an animal sanctuary and a rehousing shelter. Rosie helps take down a dog fighting ring.

Hawthorne's Investigations.

Dylan Hawthorne. Owner of Hawthorne investigations. He is extremely intelligent and will bend and break the rules as he wants. He thinks of Drake as a close friend and takes Rage's back during the Artemis war. He discovers information on Artemis, which leads to Rage discovering who she is. Dylan protects Matthieu in the Sweetness of Rage.

Davies. Hawthorne investigator. He's Hawthorne's top security expert and also does undercover work.

Davies is Hawthorne's second in command.

RCPD.

Antonio Ramirez. He is over six-foot tall and has wavy black hair, olive tanned skin. He is Mexican and has brown soft, gentle eyes. Tonio is lean-hipped and long-legged, and broad-shouldered. He is a good cop, and Drake thinks a lot of him. Ramirez brought down his previous chief, who was taking bribes from Santos. He also quit his job when he was called out on being too close to Rage, which led to a walkout from RCPD. Tonio is involved in a fiery relationship with Sophia Hawthorne. Dylan is amused at how his cousin is running the cop ragged. Tonio is classed as one of Rage even though he's not a brother, and Drake is extremely fond of Tonio.

Hernando Hawthorne/ Nando. Following in his father's footsteps, Nando became a cop. He's loyal to his family and highly respected. Nando is becoming more involved with Rage because of his cousin's relationship with them.

Justin Goldberg. Nando's partner.

Officer Bobby Lucas. An officer that is friendly with Rage MC

Officer Dan Horton. An officer that is friendly with Rage MC.

Delta Force

Lieutenant-Colonel Jacob Reeves. Jacob dedicated

his life to serving his country and commanded a Delta Force team. He had many men under his command and was loyal to them. Jacob strongly believed in never leaving a man behind and even went against a three-star general to lead a team to save his men. Jaco helps shut the dog fighting ring down and saves Calamity.

Major Gilbert Cunningham. He is a close friend of Jacob's, and Casey refers to him as Uncle. He has sparred with Casey many times, leaving her bruised but more aware of defending herself.

Washington's.

James Washington. DOB 1966. James is Gunner's older brother. James skirted the illegal side of life and is someone Santos is afraid of. He is ten years older than Gunner. James had a sister, Chloe, born when he was five. Chloe ended up dead at seventeen. Gunner was born when he was ten. James has sandy brown hair greying at the temples and the same grey eyes as Gunner. James comes to Calamity's rescue.

Adam. Adam takes over Frank's position as a bodyguard, but James holds him at arms-length. Adam also knows a lot of secrets and carries them close unless they're a threat to James. He discovers he has a son who needs a liver transplant and offers up his own. He wasn't aware Walker existed. Adam finds out his brother Jake knew and kept Walker from him. He comes to Calamity's rescue.

Jaime. He was the bar manager for James's main

club. He turns out to be Frank's son. Jaime has a daughter, Ella, who he kept hidden from people, and he understands how Frank felt. He hired a hitman to kill James, which he tried to call off, but it backfired. Jaime broke his leg in Jaime and was injured in a car crash caused by Ranson. Jaime is crazy about Mandy and is planning to marry her. He comes to Calamity's rescue.

Jason. Jason is now in charge of all the strip joints and hates it. He is married to Frankie. Jason is one of six brothers, and his Mom and Dad own Barr's Juicy Milks, a nationwide business earning billions. His grandfather Pops is still alive. Jason grew up on a farm and loves being a country boy while working at Bryant and Washington. He comes to Calamity's rescue.

The Juno Group.

Akemi. (Artemis's adopted brother). Akemi is Japanese and Artemis's adopted brother. He is tall and slender with well-defined muscles. Master Hoshi calls him his son. There are no lengths Akemi won't go to, to defend his family. He uses a Katana and is graceful and beautiful when he uses it. Akemi is an expert at hand-to-hand as well as weapons.

Simone and Butch. They are two hunters at Artemis, and they will only work with each other. Butch has special force training; he moves like a ghost, and Simone is much like Artemis in character but not in looks.

Angel. He is a member of the Juno Group and was once kidnapped by Santos and tortured. Artemis rescued him.

Other Characters.

Doc Paul. A doctor who is a friend of the club. He works at the hospital and helps save many lives and often works on Rage when they're brought in. His father was a lone biker who was well-known in South Dakota.

Doc Gibbons. Doc is an older man close to retirement. He has helped patch up Rage and Hellfire and helps look after their old ladies.

Wraith. He's called Wraith because, as big as he was, the man moves like a ghost and has become a prospect in Hellfire. Does tattoos.

Micah/Fanatic

Magic. He owns a bar out in the hills on an open stretch of road that is a biker-neutral zone. Magic doesn't allow violence in his bar nor truces to be broken in it. He's a big man, but no one knows his age. No one wants to upset Magic. He's rumoured to have buried the bodies of those who've upset him in the hills behind his bar.

Lance. President of the Fallen Warriors.

Jon. Works as a trainer for rescued dogs from dog fighting.

Kenny. He is a fully-trained vet and Jon's cousin. He

left his home state due to woman trouble.

Winnie. She was Rosie's nurse at the old clinic and followed Rosie when she opened the new one.

Chelsea. The receptionist at Rosie's old clinic.

Brett. A vet who sexually harassed Rosie, causing her to quit her job. He later tries to burn her new clinic down and is shot by Calamity and arrested.

Rex. He sexually harassed Rosie at college because she said no to a date. Calamity beats him down, and he is killed by Hayleigh.

Janine. Brett's aunt who owns half the clinic Rosie worked at.

Dr Steiner. Janine's husband owns the other half of the clinic Rosie worked at.

Hayleigh. The physiotherapist that Rosie hires to help Calamity get better.

Mrs Travis. She took Calamity under her wing when he was eleven and loved him. She was a wealthy widow who owned three well-known companies. Mrs Travis lost her husband and son in a fire. She left everything she owned to Calamity.

Clyde. Calamity's father. He abused Calamity and was captured after kidnapping and torturing Calamity. He was killed by Blaze and the others while Rosie watched.

Deirdre. Calamity's birth mother. She abused Calamity and tried to kill him while he was in the hospital. She was injected with her own poison instead.

Lawless Rogues. A now-dead MC that was one percenter's and had been around for 100 years. Clyde rode with them.

Micah. Micah is Phoe's oldest son and rides with Hellfire as a legacy prospect. He is car-mad and Calamity's best friend.

Scott Deverish. He was Mrs Travis's lawyer and now works for Calamity.

Thank you for reading Calamity. Please take a gander at the Hellfire MC Series, starting with Chance's Hell. **For** more Rage check out Rage MC, book one The Rage of the Phoenix is the beginning of the Rage MC world. Or take a peek at Washingtons, starting with James.

Also, take a gander at the Love Beyond Death series, book one of which, Oakwood Manor, is out now. And the new series of Love Beyond Death-The Inns begins with The Jekyll and Hyde. If you enjoyed this book, please leave a review at,

Goodreads and Amazon

Please remember your reviews are so important to me!

Thank you!

Elizabeth.

Printed in Great Britain
by Amazon

17647003R00159